UNEXPECTEDLY IN LOVE

THE SHERBROOKES
BOOK 1

CHRISTINA TETREAULT

Unexpectedly In Love ©2023 by Christina Tetreault
Published by Christina Tetreault
Cover Designer: Amanda Walker
Editing: Hot Tree Editing
Proofreading: Hot Tree Editing

Digital ISBN: 979-8-9865744-1-7

Print ISBN: 979-8-9865744-2-4

ONE

"I ORDERED MY TICKET TO THE BACHELOR AUCTION THIS morning. You should come with me this time. It'll be fun. We can turn it into a girls-only weekend. Attend the auction Saturday night and then head to New York City on Sunday and do some shopping or maybe catch a show."

Victoria Sherbrooke, better known as Tory to her friends and family, picked up her laptop and typed *what shows are in NYC* into her favorite search engine, even though Ivy hadn't agreed yet.

"We haven't had one in ages, and this might be the last time we can do it," Tory continued before Ivy could respond.

"Tory, I'm engaged. So why would I go to a bachelor auction?"

"Because it's for a great cause, and you don't have to bid on anyone. I didn't at the last one. And it was a lot of fun watching women try to outbid each other. I told you the story about Tasha Marshall, right?"

Actually, she'd found some of the women's behavior downright hilarious, and she wasn't lying, it was for a good cause.

All the money raised at the auction would go to the Helping Hands Foundation, an organization founded during the Great

Depression by Tory's great-grandmother Margaret Sherbrooke to help provide for homeless families. Today, the foundation, whose headquarters were still located in Providence, Rhode Island, supported a wide range of programs around the country. About three years ago, it had held its first bachelor auction. The event had been such a tremendous success the foundation decided to hold another one this fall.

“Yes. And I wish I'd been there that night. Tasha has never been my favorite person, and you know it.”

Ivy and Tasha had attended the same high school. Tory hadn't known Ivy at the time, but Ivy had shared with her that at the beginning of her sophomore year, she'd started dating Tasha's ex-boyfriend. Unfortunately, Tasha hadn't been ready to see the guy move on, and she'd spent the rest of the year trying to come between them while at the same time making Ivy's life hell. Even though it had happened years ago, the two women still didn't like each other. Unfortunately, both often found themselves at many of the same social events, so they occasionally had to not only interact but be civil to each other.

“You never know. She might embarrass herself again. You don't want to miss that, do you?”

Usually, Tory wouldn't enjoy seeing someone embarrass themselves or hope they did it again. Neither would Ivy. But Tasha wasn't like most people, and she usually brought it on herself. Not only that, but if the possibility of Tasha making a fool out of herself got Ivy to agree to come, Tory wasn't above using it, especially since Ivy might say now that they could continue going on their girls-only trips, but it might change once she was married.

“I'll even order the ticket for you.” Ivy didn’t need Tory purchasing her a ticket, but every little bit helped when it came to convincing a person.

Tory scrolled through the list of shows either currently in New York or that would be there soon. She loved going to the theater, and since she hadn't seen a show in at least nine months, she expected to see at least one that interested her. But, surprisingly, today, that wasn't the case. In fact, the only performance that mildly appealed to her was *The Nutcracker*. But it wasn't opening until the end of November, and the fundraiser was on November 1, making it not even an option.

"It's a tempting thought, but I can't go with you. The wedding is in about a month, and I still have a lot to do. But don't worry, we'll still be able to do our girls' weekends away. We've been doing them longer than I've known Preston, and he knows it. He also knows if he asks me to stop going, I'll say the same about his golfing trips with his friends, and you know how much he enjoys those."

You had to bring that up. "Please don't remind me about the wedding," Tory said, leaning her head against the sofa and closing her eyes.

It wasn't that she had anything against marriage or weddings, which was a good thing since, thanks to her numerous cousins, she'd been to more weddings than the average person in the past five years. And honestly, unlike many people who attended one and counted the minutes until they could leave, she enjoyed them. Often, they gave her a chance to catch up with people she hadn't seen in a while. And it wasn't that she didn't want to see Ivy get married or that she disliked Ivy's fiancé, Preston Turner. Preston was perfect for her former college roommate. Nope, Grant Castillo, Preston's best man and cousin, was the problem.

Tory had known Grant, the only son of her dad's close friend, her entire life. However, they'd only gotten romantically involved earlier in the year. Much to Grant's disappointment, as well as that of both families, she'd broken things off in August. Ever since then, Grant had been trying to get back together. And when he wasn't reaching out to her, one of her parents brought up the topic. Her parents simply refused to accept that she and Grant wouldn't someday be married.

If Ivy were having a wedding like the one her cousin Brett had this summer, Grant's presence wouldn't be as much of an issue, even though they were both in the wedding party, because she could tolerate anyone for a few hours—a helpful quality considering how often she found herself at either fundraisers or her parents' various dinner parties. But her friend's wedding wouldn't be anything like Brett and Jennifer's. Or any other wedding she'd ever attended, for that matter.

Ivy and Preston had planned a beach wedding in Puerto Rico; not only that, they had an itinerary of events lined up for the week leading up to the big day. As the maid of honor, Tory couldn't just fly in the night before the wedding and then leave right after the reception. Nope, Ivy expected her on hand with the rest of the wedding party for all the fun—or, in Tory's case, all the torture.

"Is Grant bugging you again?" Ivy asked.

Opening her eyes, Tory stared at the ceiling and, for at least the hundredth time, wished she'd never agreed to join Grant for dinner in the first place. "'Again' gives the impression he stopped."

"Last time we talked, it'd been over a week since he contacted you. I thought maybe he'd given up and moved on."

"I wish. He came to the dinner party my parents held last week. I assumed his parents would be there. Mom and Dad always invite them to those things, and I can't remember them ever not going. But if I'd known Grant would be there too, I would've skipped it. He stayed glued to my side all night. He left me alone only when I went to the bathroom. When I walked out, I expected him to be waiting by the door for me." She'd escaped to the bathroom as often as she could too.

"Your parents had to know he was coming. They should've given you a heads-up when they invited you," Ivy said with annoyance.

Ever since she'd learned Tory's parents were pressuring her to give Grant another chance, Ivy hadn't been the biggest fan of Benjamin and Shannon Sherbrooke. Her former roommate wasn't shy about letting Tory know it, either. And if the tables were reversed, Tory would feel the same way about Ivy's parents. But, of course, Ivy's parents would never be able to agree on a man for their only daughter. Tory had never met two people who disagreed more than Christian and Amber Nelson. How they remained married should be considered a modern mystery of the world.

"We both know why they didn't. But I should've asked when Mom called me. It's not uncommon for her to invite him. Next time I'll remember to ask who else will be there before I agree or not go at all." As much as the lack of information bothered her, Tory couldn't put all the blame on her parents.

"I don't know why you always go anyway."

"Funny. Neither do I."

She loved her parents, but watching a race between two snails would be more exciting than one of their dinner parties. For some reason, though, she usually went, unlike her two siblings. Even before her older brother, Adam, moved back to the East Coast, the only party their parents held that he attended was their annual holiday party in December. Tyler, her younger brother, didn't even always go to that, and he lived nearly as close to their parents as she did.

Or rather, she had.

The day after her parents' gathering, she'd finalized the sale of her house in California and hopped a plane to the other side of the country. For the past seven days, she'd called the Sherbrooke Copley Square in Boston home. Tomorrow afternoon, she'd sign all the paperwork for her new condo and move in. Well, more like "officially" move in. Since her cousin Alec owned the condo she was purchasing, he'd allowed her to start moving in her stuff early. The movers had delivered her things two days ago, and she'd started unpacking yesterday. So far, she hadn't gotten very far, which was why she'd decided to spend one last night at the hotel rather than at the condo, even though Alec wouldn't have minded if she had.

"I don't know how I'll make it through the week if he acts as he did at my parents' house while we're in Puerto Rico." She hadn't even stepped foot on the island yet, and she already pictured Grant waiting outside her hotel room each morning so he could escort her to breakfast or whatever event Ivy had planned for the day.

"Do you want me to ask Preston to talk to him?"

It wasn't the first time Ivy had made the offer. "No, I don't think it'll help."

"It doesn't hurt to try, and who knows, he might finally get the message and leave you alone."

There Tory disagreed. People could be weird when third parties stuck their noses where they didn't belong. Grant might brush off such a conversation with his cousin. Or he might get angry. As frustrated as she was with Grant, she didn't want to cause a rift between him and Preston, especially not with the wedding right around the corner.

"The only thing that might get the message through his thick skull is if I announce I'm engaged. Even then, he might not accept it. I'm pretty sure my parents wouldn't. They really want to join our families." Although why both parties wanted it escaped her. It wasn't like either needed a boost in their social standings, and money wasn't an issue for either family.

"Hey, that's not a bad idea."

With their conversation about as far away from a girls' weekend in New York as you could get, Tory set her laptop down. "You want me to tell Grant I'm engaged? He'd never believe me. And I wouldn't blame him. I wouldn't believe me either."

Maybe if seven or eight months had passed since she broke things off, she could convince him she'd met and fallen for someone else. But not after only two months, especially since she hadn't been seen with anyone else.

"No, that would look too forced. But if you arrive in Puerto Rico for the wedding with a boyfriend, Grant might accept that you don't want anything to do with him. At the very least, I think he'd leave you alone while you're there. And afterward, you'll be on opposite sides of the country again, so he'll never know the difference. It's not like I can't add one more person to the guest list."

Tory believed in looking outside the box for solutions. However, Ivy's suggestion was not only outside the box but outside this reality. "I love your idea, Ivy. Really, I do. Only it has one teeny tiny hole in it. I don't have a boyfriend. I haven't even been out with anyone since before Grant. So who am I supposed to bring with me?"

Tory had plenty of friends who'd help her out if she ever needed it. But, unfortunately, they were all women, and the only men she knew who'd step up if she needed them were related to her—making them useless in this situation.

"Unless you know a place where I can rent a boyfriend for the week, don't bother adding another person to your guest list."

"Nope, but you do. Well, maybe not rent a boyfriend but at least meet a possible candidate. You're going to a bachelor auction. The keyword in that sentence is bachelor, my friend. I'm looking at the website now. There are going to be twelve very single men there."

She'd tossed around the idea of bidding on a bachelor just because it might be fun and the money went to a good cause, but she had yet to decide. She'd logged onto the website long enough to purchase her ticket last week but hadn't bothered to see who'd be parading across the stage in November.

"Ivy, the men participating agreed to take the highest bidder on four romantic dates. They didn't agree to pretend to be someone's boyfriend and go away for a week."

Sure, the men were all single, but that didn't mean they were interested in anything more than what they signed up for.

"Two of your cousins met their wives at the last one. So maybe you'll bid on Mr. Right, and he won't have to pretend."

Ivy wasn't entirely correct there. Yes, Scott had the auction to thank for bringing Paige into his life. However, Derek and his wife, Brooklyn, had been friends long before she outbid everyone else and embarrassed the heck out of Tasha in the process. Tory saw no point in correcting Ivy, though, because, at the end of the day, it didn't matter. The auction had played a role in both of their relationships.

"That's about as likely as it snowing on your wedding day." Mr. Right might be out there, and she might meet him someday, but it wouldn't be at next month's fundraiser.

"Hey, if you pick the right bachelor, you never know. Even if he's not the one, he might be willing to help you out in exchange for something." Once Ivy got an idea in her head, she didn't like to let it go. Clearly, she wasn't ready to give up on her crazy proposal.

"Such as? And if you say sex, I'm hanging up now."

Some people would help her in exchange for an all-expenses trip to Puerto Rico. But not those who would be strutting across the stage next month. If they wanted a trip somewhere, they could all afford it.

"No, not sex."

"Then what?" Tory couldn't think of a single thing that would entice her to do what Ivy suggested she ask a stranger to do.

"I don't know. At least one of those men probably has political aspirations. Perhaps you can promise to endorse him or make a hefty donation to his campaign. We both know how much the Sherbrooke name helps in politics."

Tory knew all too well how much clout the Sherbrooke name carried. She was convinced it was one reason Grant, who saw himself in the California Governor's mansion or even the White House someday, refused to accept they had no future together. She knew it was the reason Luke, her ex-fiancé, had asked her to marry him. And Ivy was right. Given the type of individuals participating, there was a high probability at least one saw politics in their future. But she couldn't publicly back someone or donate money without knowing his stance on issues, even if it would keep Grant from bothering her while at the wedding.

"Even if I were comfortable doing either, he'd have to intend to run soon. I doubt anyone would be willing to help me now if his campaign is years away. Do you have any other brilliant suggestions, oh wise one?"

"Hey, I've gotten us this far. It's your turn to contribute."

She wasn't sold on the idea of bringing a fake boyfriend to the wedding. But for now, she'd play along with Ivy's scheme. After all, she had nothing to lose by continuing this crazy conversation.

"Fine, let me think." Tory drummed her fingertips against her leg as she stared out the window. "Well, it's a fundraising event, right? So if they're willing to participate in it, maybe they're passionate about other causes too."

"And you can offer to donate to one of their choosing in exchange for their help," Ivy said, completing Tory's train of thought. After living together for four years, they knew each other well.

The whole idea was a crazy long shot, but desperate times called for desperate measures. And unfortunately, she didn't see herself getting involved with anyone between now and the wedding. "Exactly."

"Let's go through the list and decide on a few possibilities. Do you have the website up?"

I've got nothing better to do.

"Give me a second," Tory said, reaching for the laptop and typing in the website address.

A moment later, the official page for the event appeared. Along with the details about the evening and the foundation, there was a page showcasing headshots of each man and their short bios. Many of the faces she recognized, and a few she considered acquaintances.

"Wow, I can't believe Henry Blakey is doing it again." She didn't know the man personally, but she'd seen him at various events, including the last auction. "Either he's a big supporter of the foundation, or he really enjoyed the last one."

"If even half of what the media says about him is true, he doesn't make your list," Ivy said.

On that, she agreed. The media portrayed Henry as the classic womanizing bad boy. But, based on the treatment her cousins and brothers had received over the years from the media, she knew none of it might be true or it all might be. In this case, the truth didn't matter, though. No one, including Grant, would ever believe she was dating someone with Henry's reputation.

"Who else can we cro—" Ivy stopped suddenly. "Shoot, Mom is at the door. I forgot she was stopping by. I'll call you back later and help you finish your list if you want."

"Don't worry about it. I've got it. Say hi to your mom for me."

"Will do. And let me know if you decide on anyone."

After ending the call, Tory answered a text message from another friend before turning her attention back to the laptop. She might not go through with Ivy's half-baked idea, but it didn't hurt to see what bachelors would be there in November. And it wasn't like she had anything better to do tonight.

Tory skipped the bios of the following two men. She was as acquainted with Kevin Casella as she ever wanted to be. She'd never met Bradford Mulligan, but by all accounts, he was a great guy who donated to various charitable organizations. So, for now, she'd put him in the maybe category.

Scrolling down the page, she paused at Junior Morris. Anyone with two eyes and a pulse would when a picture of him popped up. The man was incredibly handsome and rumored to be one of the nicest players in the NFL. Unfortunately, the last part was the problem. She had a rule about not dating professional athletes, no matter the sport they played or how great a person they were rumored to be. Grant knew that too, so he'd never believe they were dating, no matter how hard she tried to sell it.

With another bachelor crossed off, she moved on to the next one. Again, like the first four, she recognized his name and face.

"Duncan Ferguson, how did you end up part of this?" Tory scanned the bio alongside the picture.

It would be a stretch to say her cousin Alec's friend Duncan was an acquaintance. But she remembered him from high school. She'd been a junior the year Duncan and her cousin started at Phillips Exeter Academy. She knew little about his life these days, but she'd never heard anything negative attached to his name.

For now, she'd add him to the need-to-gather-more-information list too.

Five minutes later, her mental list contained four names. And out of them, Clay Bentley was the only one she'd never at least heard of before tonight.

"All right, Mr. Bentley, let's see what we can find out about you."

After typing his name, she reached for her tea. Before she even took a sip, several results appeared on the screen, and she opened the first one.

A photo of Clay alone appeared. Although a great shot, her eyes zeroed in on one further down the page. In this one, Clay and another man, who had to be his brother based on the resemblance, stood next to Gregg Miller and an attractive sixty-something-year-old woman. While she couldn't recall ever seeing any of his movies, she knew Gregg had been starring in films and television shows longer than she'd been alive. She'd never read anywhere that the well-known actor had any children, yet both men in the photo were younger versions of him.

Pictures were great, but they wouldn't give her any background on Clay, so she skipped down to the brief article.

A representative for Clay Bentley, the oldest son of Gregg Miller and his wife Nancy, announced that Clay will appear alongside Anderson Brady in *Codename Revenge*. Although this is Clay's first starring role in a major picture, it is not

his first time in front of the camera. Last year he appeared in episodes 10 and 11 of *The Runner*. And this year he played the reoccurring role of the mechanic, Jeff Winters, in the small-town drama *Coming Home*. *Codename Revenge* will begin filming in January.

Well, if any of the bachelors could pull off playing the role of her fake boyfriend, it would be an actor. And since he wasn't a household name yet, she shouldn't have to worry about fans following them around or, worse, disrupting Ivy's wedding. Unfortunately, she'd dated enough actors to know big egos could be even more of a problem than overexcited fans. She'd rather deal with Grant all week than an actor with an overinflated opinion of himself.

Since the next portion of the page focused on Anderson Brady, an actor she'd dated for a few months years ago and whom she still considered a friend, she moved on to the following site from her original search. Unlike the first one, this one provided everything from Clay's birthdate and where he'd grown up to what sports he played in school. According to the article, he and his brother grew up in Montana rather than near Hollywood because his parents didn't want their children living under the spotlight, which explained why she never realized Gregg Miller had any children. It went on to say Clay had belonged to a local 4-H chapter until he graduated from high school. Unfortunately, it didn't mention any charitable causes he supported, but hopefully, a little more digging would turn something up. For now, though, she'd leave him on the list and move on to Duncan Ferguson, the next unsuspecting bachelor.

Her phone rang as she finished typing his name. Picking it up, Tory expected to see "Mom" on the screen. They'd only spoken once since Tory left California, but Mom knew she closed on her new condo tomorrow. And if it were her mom, she'd let the call go to her voice mail and call her back later. Unlike when Adam announced he was moving, Mom hadn't supported her decision to accept a new position and start a new life three thousand miles away. At the moment, she wasn't in the mood for another lecture about what a silly decision it had been and how she should reconsider. She also didn't want to hear a long list of Grant's fine qualities or the reasons why she should give him a second chance.

Turning over the phone, Tory touched the green answer icon when she saw the name Leah. Although they'd been born two weeks apart, since they lived on opposite coasts, she had spent little time with her cousin Leah until they were fourteen and shared a dorm room at school. Within a month of living together, they'd been like sisters—something neither of them had—and they'd opted to share a room all four years at Phillips. And although Tory had a lot of good friends, she considered Leah her closest, and she knew Leah felt the same way.

These days, Leah and her husband spent most of their time in Connecticut. However, they also had a place in New York City since they both worked there and didn't always want to deal with the commute. Tory didn't blame them either. It was the main reason she'd opted for a condo in Boston rather than a neighboring town, because while she could work from home some days, she would need to make an appearance in the office. Regardless of which home Leah and Gavin stayed at, Tory's relocation would allow her to see her cousin more often, a fact she'd taken into consideration before deciding to move.

"Aren't you supposed to be on vacation?" Tory asked after greeting Leah.

While Tory loved her family and friends, she didn't want to talk to them when she was on vacation, even if part of the vacation had been to visit relatives, which had been the case for Leah and Gavin.

"We got home yesterday."

That explained the phone call tonight.

"Have you closed on the condo yet? I knew it was happening this week but couldn't remember when."

"Tomorrow afternoon."

"I'm going to my parents' this weekend. Do you want some company? I'll even help you unpack."

Unlike Tory, Leah's parents preferred to live outside Boston and deal with the traffic. During rush hour, the trip could easily take well over an hour. But assuming the weather cooperated and there were no major sporting events, one could get from their house to the city on the weekends in about thirty minutes.

"Alec let me have things delivered already, so I have started, but I'd love the extra help." Of course, if Leah were there, they'd probably do more talking than work, but so what? The world wouldn't end if it took her an extra few days to unpack. "Speaking of company, are you attending the bachelor auction next month?"

Like Ivy, Leah did not need a bachelor auction, but since her aunt was the foundation's director, it was possible she planned to attend. And Tory would find it a lot more fun if Leah were there.

"I haven't decided yet. Why?"

"I'm going. Come with me. We'll have fun."

"Sure, why not? It was entertaining last time."

Even though she'd started a potential list, Tory wasn't sure she wanted to proceed with Ivy's crazy plan. But either way, Leah might have some insight into the four men she'd put on her list of potential bachelors. "Do you know any of the men that'll be there?"

"It's possible. I haven't looked to see who is participating. Why? Thinking about bidding on someone this time?"

"Maybe. A few of them I know and would never want to go out with even once, never mind four times. It'd be nice to know a little more about the rest."

"I'll look over the website when I buy my ticket and see if I know any of them. And if I don't, Gavin might. Is there anyone in particular you are interested in?"

"Right now I'm considering Clay Bentley, Duncan Ferguson, Bradford Mulligan, and Tucker Pierce."

"I only met him once, but Tucker is a good friend of Harry. That should tell you all you need to know."

"I'm crossing him off my list as we speak."

Yep. Harry, Gavin's brother, was the biggest playboy around. Anyone who would be good friends with him wasn't the type of man she'd date.

"Good move. Clay Bentley, I've never heard of, but I know Duncan is the founder of Chat and he lives in Boston," Leah said before sharing what else she knew about him.

DUNCAN HEARD his condo door open as he placed the spinach dip he'd removed from the microwave on the counter. It was a bad idea from a security standpoint, but he always left the door unlocked when he was expecting friends. They all knew it too, so none ever bothered to ring the bell or knock.

A moment later, his best friend, Alec Sherbrooke, walked into the room carrying an overnight bag. "Which room do you want me to use?"

Until a few months ago, Alec had also called the Heritage on the Harbor Terrace home, but these days he lived on Sanborn Island. The same island Duncan had lived on until he was eleven and, in many ways, still considered home. It was also a place he frequently visited because much of his family still lived there, which was why in August he'd purchased a home there. Since Alec needed to be in Boston tomorrow, he was spending the night at Duncan's rather than at a hotel.

"You pick. It doesn't matter to me." He had two identical guest bedrooms he always kept ready for when his family visited.

Turning off the oven timer, Duncan pulled out the chicken wings and added them to the spread already on the kitchen island. While he could cook actual meals, when his friends came over, he took the easy route and went with foods that required little more than heating up and takeout. Tonight's menu included some frozen appetizers he'd bought and pizzas.

Alec wasted no time helping himself to the dip when he came back into the kitchen. “I thought Matt would already be here.”

“Me too. He left the office around five.”

They'd met their mutual friend and Duncan's business partner, Matt Sinclair, their freshman year of college. When Alec asked if he could crash at Duncan's for the night, he'd invited Matt over to watch the baseball game and play poker, two things they'd done frequently before Alec moved but not once since the spring.

“Maybe he's ditching us to spend time with Everly.”

Three weeks ago, Duncan would've said yeah, most likely. “I'm not sure he's still seeing her. He hasn't mentioned her to me in over a week, and he's been spending a lot of time here.”

Following the end of a two-year relationship, one he hadn't ended, Matt had moved into the building in January and, at first, spent more time at Duncan's place than his own. In late February, though, he'd started dating again. Now, he only hung around and raided Duncan's fridge every other day when he was between girlfriends. Unfortunately, the guy had done that three out of the last five nights—a clear sign that either Matt and Everly were no longer together or soon wouldn't be.

“No luck convincing Gianna to come with you?” Duncan asked, referring to his favorite cousin and the reason why his best friend now lived on Sanborn Island rather than a few floors above him.

Shaking his head, Alec frowned and opened a beer. “Trust me, I tried.”

He loved being right. “I told you there was no way you'd get her off the island during the week until at least mid-November.”

“If Owen hadn't called in sick for the rest of the week and Shane and Roger weren't already scheduled to have tomorrow off, she would've come with me.”

"Keep telling yourself that if it makes you feel better."

While Duncan spent his days in an office, his cousin oversaw the landscaping side of her dad's business. In addition to administrative duties, she worked alongside the company's employees. Although not the only landscaping company on the island, May Point Landscaping was the largest. And early spring through late fall was its busiest season, which meant his cousin rarely left the island during those months. When she did, it involved short weekend gateways.

"What would make me feel better is something to eat."

Alec might not live there, but Duncan didn't consider him a guest either. "Help yourself." Duncan gestured toward the food as he grabbed a plate and added some of everything to it. "I ordered pizzas too. They should be here—"

The door opened before he finished. "I'm here. The party can start." Matt's voice reached them in the kitchen, announcing his arrival.

His friend had given him too good an opening to pass up. "Thanks for the warning, so I know it's time to leave. What do you say we head over to Dwyer's and watch the game, Alec?" Duncan asked, referring to a nearby sports pub they often visited.

"You've both been looking forward to spending time with me all day, and you know it." Entering the kitchen, Matt added three pizza boxes and a six-pack of beer to the island. "The delivery guy was about to ring the bell when I got off the elevator, so I paid him."

"Thanks. I'll get them next time."

"You'll never guess who I rode the elevator up with when I got home tonight." Matt stuffed a jalapeño popper in his mouth and then piled various appetizers onto a plate.

"My fairy godmother?" Duncan went straight for the pizza. If he could only eat one food for the rest of his life, he'd pick pizza.

"You're going to wish it was."

Matt's smile told him everything he needed to know. Whoever it was, he wasn't going to like it. Unlike some of his friends, he didn't have a string of ex-girlfriends, but he had a few, and they were ex-girlfriends for a reason. Had one of them moved into the building?

"Are you going to tell me or not?" Duncan asked when Matt didn't continue, because you couldn't leave someone hanging after a statement like that.

"Lori Ann."

Next to him, Alec laughed, and Duncan suppressed the urge to stuff a chicken wing in the guy's mouth.

"I thought she was in New Orleans."

"Not anymore. The company she works for transferred her back to Boston. She moved back into the building yesterday," Matt said as he lifted his beer to his lips.

"It must be your lucky day, Duncan." Alec barely managed to keep a straight face when he commented.

"She asked about you, and when I mentioned we were playing poker tonight, she told me to say hello."

"Just what I needed."

The damn city was full of condos. So why the hell did she have to move back into this building?

Not long after he'd moved into the building two years ago, she'd purchased the condo next door to him. For some reason, she'd immediately singled him out as her new best friend, despite the number of people living in the building. Almost daily, she'd knock on his door. Sometimes she'd have baked goods for him. Other times, she just wanted to talk his ear off. It didn't seem to matter what he said or how short he kept their conversation; she kept knocking on his door or sending him text messages. So he'd been beyond ecstatic when she moved to New Orleans last year.

"I'm surprised she didn't ask if she could join us," Alec said.

"Told her we were meeting at Jim's place," Matt answered around a mouthful of food.

"I owe you one." Considering that Matt's cousin Jim lived in

Dallas, it'd be a little difficult for them to play poker there tonight.

"Don't worry, I'll remember. So, Alec, how long are you sticking around?" Matt asked as he reached for his beer.

"Just the night. I hope to make it back to Portsmouth for the four o'clock ferry home."

"Too bad. I've got an extra ticket to the basketball game. I know Duncan won't want to go."

Matt was right there. Duncan could watch baseball every day. Even an occasional football game he enjoyed. He wanted nothing to do with basketball. He'd prefer a trip to the Department of Motor Vehicles to a basketball game.

Following Matt's lead, Alec filled his plate. "Everly can't go?"

"She decided to extend her trip to Miami." A combination of frustration and annoyance permeated Matt's words.

They'd been friends long enough that Duncan knew Matt's displeasure stemmed from more than the fact his girlfriend had extended her vacation.

"Indefinitely," Matt added before he walked out of the kitchen. "She's moving in with someone she reconnected with while down there. She said they dated on and off when they used to work together."

He'd expected Matt to say they were no longer together, but not that. "That's rough, man. I'm sorry."

Before joining his friends at the table, Duncan switched on the baseball game. Tonight was the third game in the Wild Card series between the Red Sox and the Yankees. Whoever won tonight clinched a spot in the playoffs. If the game were being played in Boston instead of New York, Duncan would be watching from inside Fenway Park rather than from his living room. But, unfortunately, that wasn't the case, so he'd have to settle for watching it this way.

"Whatever. Shit happens." Matt shrugged half-heartedly and took a drink.

Duncan glanced at Alec, and judging by his expression, Alec was thinking the same thing he was. The situation bothered Matt a lot more than he wanted them to think.

"Maybe you should reconsider and join Duncan in the auction. If I call my aunt, I know she'll happily squeeze you into the lineup."

"Thanks, but I'll let Duncan have the spotlight and watch from the audience."

He knew it was asking too much for his friends to stay as far away from the Helping Hands Bachelor auction as possible.

"Gianna and I'll be there too. We're looking forward to it."

I'm sure you are. Of course, if Alec were the one up on the stage, Duncan wouldn't miss it either. He'd even record the evening so he could show it to everyone they knew.

Matt paused in dealing the cards. "You know, I don't think we've gotten together since the night Duncan made that bet with you."

"Yeah, you're right, Matt. We haven't," Alec said.

"Worst idea I have ever had." If he'd kept his big trap shut that night, his name wouldn't be listed on the bachelor auction's website.

"I disagree with you. It worked out great for me. I've never been happier," Alec said as he picked up his cards. "Gianna would disagree with you too."

When he'd proposed the bet, Duncan had been sure he'd be the winner and Alec would be the one waltzing across the stage in November. But, unfortunately, Alec had not only won but also fallen for Gianna—not that he wasn't happy for the couple. After all, Alec was his best friend and Gianna his favorite cousin. Despite that, he would've preferred to win the bet, see Alec auctioned off, and then have the two of them meet and fall in love.

"Have you decided what you and the winner will do?" Alec asked.

"Nope."

He was finding it incredibly difficult to come up with ideas for four dates when he didn’t know who they'd be with. If the winner turned out to be a seventy-something-year-old woman, she wouldn't enjoy a dance club—at least he'd never met a seventy-year-old that would. And, if the winner were anything like his younger sister, a hike followed by a romantic picnic wouldn't cut it.

“The auction is in about two weeks. Cutting it a little close, aren't you?” Matt asked, lifting a slice of pizza to his mouth.

He didn't need Matt or anyone else to remind him when the auction was. “Don't remind me.”

“Hey, it might not be as bad as you think. My brother and cousin wouldn't be married if not for the auction,” Alec said.

It was easy for Alec to say that. He wasn't the one about to have random women bidding on him while he stood there in a monkey suit. “No. It'll be worse.”

TWO

November

Tory reached for her lipstick just as someone knocked on her hotel suite door. While she could've stayed with a relative in Providence, she'd opted to stay at the Bellevue Hotel, one of Sherbrooke Enterprises' oldest hotels in the country. It was also where the bachelor auction was being held again this year, making it the logical place to stay.

"I'm almost ready," Tory said after letting Leah into the suite and hugging her.

Leah placed her clutch on a nearby table and sat down. "No rush. I'm a few minutes early. I left home right after Gavin and Erin headed out."

"What are they up to tonight?"

Leah's stepdaughter lived in Providence with her mom, so Leah and her husband had a place in the city too, so that on the weekends when Erin was with them, they didn't waste their time together driving back and forth to Connecticut. Tonight's auction fell on a weekend when Erin was staying with her dad and Leah.

"They're going roller-skating and then for ice cream."

Tory had learned how to rollerblade but had always done that either outside her parents' house or around campus when in high school. "There are still places around where you can go roller-skating?" She knew such places had once been popular but assumed they'd all gone out of business decades ago.

"I didn't think there were any either, but there's one about twenty minutes from here that Erin loves. Believe it or not, the place even has an arcade."

"Learn something new every day," Tory said before stepping into the bathroom so she could finish her makeup.

"Are you heading back to Boston tomorrow morning?"

"Yeah. I thought about staying Sunday night, but I have a lot of work waiting for me at home."

Although she'd known the CEO of the magazine and her daughter for years, as the new marketing director, Tory couldn't take days off already without a good reason. And taking a day off because she wanted to spend the weekend in Providence and visit with family wasn't a good reason in her book.

"That stinks. I was going to invite you over tomorrow night. Brett and Jennifer are around, so they're coming by for dinner. Curt and Taylor are coming too."

She hadn't seen either of Leah's brothers and their wives since the summer and, at another time, would've enjoyed catching up with them.

"Next time." Now that she lived in New England, she'd be able to see her East Coast cousins a lot more.

Lipstick on, Tory checked her reflection a final time before adding the tube to her purse and turning off the bathroom light. "I'm all set if you are?"

While traditional and much faster elevators transported guests between floors, most visitors opted to use the Bellevue Hotel's iconic glass elevator when heading up to the grand ballroom on the top level. Rather than join the trio of exquisitely dressed women waiting for it now, though, Tory and Leah opted for the set of elevators located down the hallway.

"By the way, your gown is gorgeous. Is it a Jolie?"

Tory nodded and pressed the button for the top floor. "It was part of her fall collection last year. I bought it for my parents' holiday party but ended up with the flu and couldn't go." She'd considered looking for something new for tonight but ran out of time. And since she'd never worn this one, it seemed like the next best thing.

Beautifully dressed women of all ages and a handful of men in tuxedos mingled in the lobby near the grand ballroom doors when Tory and Leah stepped off the elevator. Many of the people, Tory knew. Those that she didn't, Leah did.

And unsurprisingly, they'd only taken a handful of steps before one of Leah's friends, a woman Tory was acquainted with, waved them over. For the next several minutes, Leah's friend filled them in on her recent divorce and trip back into the dating world. To anyone watching, it would appear as though Tory was paying attention. But in reality, she was mentally debating for the umpteenth time whether to proceed with Ivy's idea or not. Ivy still insisted it was a solid plan and worth trying. Some of the time, Tory agreed. But almost as often, she decided it wasn't worth the potential headaches that might result from it. For the moment, she was again leaning toward giving it a try.

"Do either of you know Duncan Ferguson or Clay Bentley? I'm thinking about bidding on them tonight," Leah's friend asked, pulling Tory away from her thoughts and to the conversation.

"I know Duncan is my cousin's friend, and he went to school with us." Leah gestured between herself and Tory. "But I don't remember the last time I saw him. And until I saw his name and picture on the website, I'd never heard of Clay Bentley," Leah replied before glancing at Tory. "Do you know Clay?"

"I've never met him, but I read he's Gregg Miller's son. He is going to be starring in a movie with Anderson sometime next year."

"Interesting. My mom loves Gregg Miller. I don't think a movie or television show exists that he's been on and she hasn't seen." Leah's friend waved to someone across the lobby. "My mom and sister just got off the elevator. I can't wait to tell her whose son will be up on the stage tonight," she continued before touching Leah on the arm. "Let's get together soon."

Tory watched her potential competition walk away. Maybe she should've included more than two bachelors on her final list.

They stopped to chat with people three more times before entering the hotel's grand ballroom. Like the rest of the hotel, the room showcased the grandeur of a different era, and if Tory had been in charge, she would've selected a more contemporary location for the event. While she couldn't deny the ballroom was beautiful, it seemed better suited to hosting more elegant events, such as weddings.

Like in the lobby, she recognized many people already seated. One particular person she hadn't seen in months. "I'm going to say hello to Milan. What table are we at? I'll meet you there."

"Three. If someone comes by taking drink orders, do you want me to order you anything?"

"Sure. Get me whatever you're having." Her cousin knew what Tory liked.

A few years older than her, Milan Novak was a highly sought-after model who'd appeared in some of the biggest runway shows in the world. And when she wasn't modeling a designer's most recent creations, she was posing for magazine covers. She'd first met Milan about two years ago when she'd been dating Tory's older brother. And even after Milan and Adam went their separate ways, they'd stayed friends. But since Milan always seemed to be off to either some photo shoot or an exotic gateway, they hadn't seen each other in a while. At the moment, Milan was alone. Tory knew from past experiences that wouldn't last. And before Milan's mom, Scarlet, who usually joined her daughter at social events like this, showed up, she wanted to at least say hello. Scarlet Novak was a former model turned talent mogul and, to put it nicely, a difficult person. When possible, Tory preferred to avoid her. Milan's father was even worse.

Pulling out the empty chair next to Milan, Tory sat. "How are you?"

"Never better. You?"

"Still settling in, but overall, I'm doing well."

"That's right. I forgot you were moving to Boston. How do you like the city so far?"

"It's growing on me." While she missed some things about California, she was coming to love her new home. "I meant to call and ask if you were attending tonight."

Smiling, Milan picked up her cocktail. "I had too much fun last time to miss it this year."

"Do you plan on bidding or just watching this time?" Tory asked.

Unlike Tory, Milan had not only bid on a bachelor but walked away with Ryan Keene, a quarterback in the NFL. Despite the way their relationship had started, they'd ended up dating for nine months before going their separate ways.

"Just watching is no fun. And I already know who I'm bidding on. Right now, my first choice is Junior Morris."

Wow, big surprise. Milan had a thing for professional athletes, and Tory had seen her linked to several over the years.

Opening the fundraiser's program, Milan flipped through the pages. "But Tucker Pierce is a close second, followed by Duncan Ferguson and Bradford Mulligan." Milan turned the program so that Tory could see Tucker's glossy headshot and bio. "What about you? Just watching again this year, or are you going to have a little fun?"

Getting into a bidding war with a stranger was one thing. Going head-to-head with a friend was another. "No, I'm bidding tonight."

"Good for you. After all, the worst thing that happens is someone outbids you and you go home empty-handed." Milan shrugged one bare shoulder.

Tory disagreed there. In her book, it'd be far worse to win and then have the guy turn out to be a complete jerk. But she wasn't going to start a debate with her friend.

"I know you'd never be interested in Junior, but if you're considering anyone on my list, just say the word, and I won't bid on them."

Milan might have her quirks, but she was a good friend. "The only one I'm thinking about from your list is Duncan Ferguson," Tory replied.

"Well, you have one less person to compete with now." Then, closing the program, Milan placed it on the table. "I'm going to be in the area all month. So let's plan on getting together soon."

Tory spotted Milan's mom and her sister Paris walking toward the table. "Sounds great. I'll call you. Good luck tonight." Standing up, Tory grabbed her clutch and fundraiser program off the table.

"You too."

She got pulled into two other brief conversations, and by the time she reached table number three, there was only one empty chair.

"Bachelor number five," the woman seated next to Alec said as Tory pulled out the chair next to Leah. She was the only person at the table Tory wasn't somehow related to; she'd seen the woman at Brett's wedding in the summer. But, unfortunately, she couldn't recall her name.

"What about number five?" Tory asked. "I'm planning to bid on him. And, if I don't win, I might try for number eight."

"Duncan is my cousin and a friend of Alec's," the woman answered.

"I knew Duncan and Alec were friends. We all went to high school together. But I didn't realize he was your cousin."

"Gianna tries to keep it a secret. I would too if Duncan was my cousin," Alec, the only man at the table, said.

"I can sympathize with you, Gianna. I prefer people don't know I'm related to Alec." Leah nudged Tory's arm. "You never tell anyone either, do you?"

Tory shook her head and picked up her water glass. "Not unless I have absolutely no other choice."

"Since clearly no one will miss me, I'm going to see how Duncan is holding up. I'll be back."

"Tell him I said hi and good luck," Gianna said.

After kissing Gianna on the cheek, he stood. "Will do."

Other than Alec, if anyone in the room knew Duncan well, it would be his cousin. And since Gianna was sitting right across the table, Tory wasn't going to waste the opportunity to ask her some questions. There was only so much you could learn from the internet. So Tory waited until her cousin left before speaking.

"Gianna, if Duncan wasn't your cousin, is he the type of person you'd want to go out with?"

LIKE THE REST of tonight's sacrifices, Duncan arrived forty-five minutes ago. And since the organizers of tonight's hell wanted to keep the bachelors out of sight until they took the stage, a foundation employee had immediately escorted them to an empty room adjacent to the ballroom. After a brief presentation regarding how the evening would proceed, Courtney, the fundraiser's director, thanked them for taking part and then left them alone.

Now six men were playing cards while discussing the football games tomorrow, and four others were having a heated conversation about politics. Duncan wanted nothing to do with either of the groups.

"You look like you're as happy as I am to be here."

Duncan couldn't recall the man's name, but he'd seen his picture on the fundraiser's website.

"My name's Clay," the dark-haired man said, extending his hand.

"Duncan. Yeah, I can think of a lot better ways to spend a Saturday night," he replied as he shook Clay's hand. "Sounds like you didn't willingly sign up for this, either."

Clay's scowl confirmed his guess. "Hell no. Because it's for charity, my agent thought it was a good way for me to get some positive publicity. My father agreed. Considering Gregg Miller's career, I'd be an idiot not to listen to him."

The actor's career spanned more than thirty years, so if anyone could give good advice, it would be him. "He has been mildly successful," Duncan said, smiling for the first time all night.

"That's one way to put it. So how did you end up here?"

"I lost a bet." Duncan frowned as he mentally kicked himself in the ass for the hundredth time this week.

"That's rough. At least I get something out of participating. I heard this is Henry Blakey's second time doing this. You'd think once was bad enough." Clay gestured toward the table where Henry sat dealing cards.

Duncan would never consider Henry a friend, but the man did a lot for various charities. "Henry supports a bunch of charities, so that's probably why he agreed to come back this year."

"I'd think writing a check would be easier and far less painful."

Before he could agree, a hotel employee approached with Clay's drink.

"Thank you," Clay said, accepting the martini glass.

Rather than walk away, the employee asked, "Can I bring you something, sir?"

Why not? He needed to pass the time and wasn't driving anywhere tonight. "I'll have a whiskey sour."

"Make that two, please," Alec said as he walked up behind him.

"They'll let anyone in here tonight," Duncan said in lieu of a proper greeting.

He realized if Alec had lost the bet and was the one about to go on stage, he'd be here to watch the night unfold too. Still, he wished Alec and Gianna were at home watching television and eating pizza. He'd even asked his cousin to reconsider coming, because if anyone would've been able to get Alec to stay home, it would be her. But, not surprisingly, Gianna had refused and then reminded Duncan that he had himself to blame for his predicament. Like he needed to be reminded.

"It helps when you know people." Alec slapped him on the shoulder. "So, how are you doing?"

How do you think? "Just wonderful. You know how much I've been looking forward to this event."

"Gianna will be relieved when I tell her that. She was worried you were miserable back here. By the way, she says hello," Alec replied before turning his attention toward Clay and introducing himself.

"Clay's about as happy about being here as I am," Duncan commented as the two men shook hands.

If Alec's smile got any bigger, he could play the role of the Cheshire Cat. "You should both think of it this way. All the money raised tonight is for a worthwhile cause."

His friend wasn't wrong there. He just would've preferred to make a monetary donation to the Helping Hands Foundation, as he did with other charities.

The hotel employee returned with their drinks, and Alec waited until he left before speaking again. "Duncan, you'll be glad to know at least one woman in the audience is thinking about bidding on you."

Duncan placed a hand over his heart. "Thank you. I feel so much better knowing that."

Before he could ask if it was anyone he knew, two employees entered with meals for the bachelors.

"Looks like they're starting to serve dinner. Maybe you should return to your table and join your better half."

"I'll catch up with you later." Alec stepped away but then stopped. "By the way, I'm proposing to Gianna tonight."

Before Duncan could get a word out, his friend walked away.

THREE

When Tory had told Milan she intended to bid tonight, she'd honestly still been teetering on the fence. But once Milan promised not to throw her hat in the ring when Duncan came on stage, Tory was left with no other choice. So now, as the hotel employees served dessert and coffee, she surveyed the room and wondered who her competition might be.

"Finally, the show is about to get started."

Alec's comment drew her attention toward the front of the room as the foundation's director, Marilyn Belmont, and her daughter, who was in charge of tonight's fundraiser, walked on the stage set up for the event.

Much like at the last auction, Marilyn stepped behind the podium first. It didn't take long for the various conversations to stop and all eyes to turn in her direction.

"Thank you all for being here tonight. For more than seventy years, the Helping Hands Foundation has worked to improve the lives of others. It wouldn't be able to do that without the help and support of each and every one of you." Applause broke out, and Marilyn paused in her speech. "And now I'll hand things off to Courtney."

While Marilyn exited the stage, Courtney adjusted the microphone behind the podium. "As the director said, the foundation wouldn't be able to help others without your support, so thank you again for being here."

More applause filled the ballroom, and Courtney waited until it stopped before speaking. "Tonight, we have twelve bachelors participating in the auction. Their names and bios are all listed in the program. Each gentleman will take the winning bidder out on four romantic dates. Everyone can place as many bids as they wish; however, if your bid is accepted, you cannot bid on any of the remaining bachelors. Now, let's meet our first bachelor." Applause once again forced Courtney to pause and wait before she could continue.

"Henry Blakey grew up in Albany, New York, but spent every summer with his grandparents in Franklin, Tennessee."

As soon as Courtney announced his name, Henry appeared on the stage.

"For his sixth birthday, he received his first guitar from his grandpa Joe, and he hasn't stopped playing since. When he's not on tour with his band, Henry divides his time between Nashville and New York City," Courtney continued.

"Did you know Henry was originally from Albany, New York?" Since his band was one of country music's biggest names, Tory had assumed he'd grown up in a place where the style was a little more popular.

"Not until I read his bio on the website," Leah answered.

"For their first date, Henry and the winning bidder will see a Broadway show and then enjoy a romantic dinner at Le Cinq," Courtney continued as Henry walked the entire length of the stage. When he reached the far end, he stopped, waved, and then returned to stand closer to the podium.

"This evening we will start the bidding at five thousand dollars," Courtney said.

Immediately, a woman seated two tables down from Tory raised her auction paddle.

"I have five thousand dollars; can I get eight?" Courtney asked.

The auctioning of the next three bachelors followed a similar script. Courtney read from the bio each man submitted, shared what he planned for the first of their four dates, and then started the bidding. So far, the largest sum, forty thousand dollars, had been dished out for Junior Morris. And much to Tory's shock, Milan hadn't been the winner despite her best efforts.

Tory sipped her wine and watched as a woman who appeared to be in her early forties walked on stage to claim Junior. Like each of the three previous couples had, they shared a kiss and posed for the photographer from the Providence Gazette before exiting together.

Across from her, Alec rubbed his hands together and smiled. "Finally."

"You might be a little too excited, considering he's your best friend," Gianna said before Tory could say something along the same lines.

"We both know Duncan would act the same way if it was me up on that stage tonight, Gi."

Tory didn't know about Duncan, but Alec's older brothers and male cousins certainly would be acting in a similar manner if Alec was about to be auctioned off. Heck, his sister might too.

"Our next bachelor this evening is Duncan Ferguson."

As soon as Courtney said his name, Duncan walked out on stage, and she continued with his introduction—not that Tory needed to hear it. She'd not only read it, but she'd learned whatever she could about him from the internet. She'd almost called Alec too, but decided it would be too awkward of a conversation.

"Once again, we will start the bidding at five thousand dollars," Courtney said.

Well, here goes nothing. Crossing her fingers, Tory raised her auction paddle.

"I have five thousand. Can I get eight?" Courtney asked, sticking with the same routine she'd used so far tonight.

At the table next to them, Tasha Marshall raised her paddle.

"He's in trouble now," Leah said before she sipped her water.

"Why?" Gianna asked.

"Remember the conversation about Tasha Marshall at Curt's house? That's her." Alec tilted his head toward the other table.

"And there is no way I'm losing to her," Tory said, putting up her paddle before Courtney finished asking for a higher bid.

Seeing the auction paddle, Courtney gestured in Tory's direction. "I now have ten thousand. Is anyone willing to go to twelve?"

Before Tasha could raise her paddle again, an older woman at table number two jumped into the bidding war.

Just great. More competition. Tory might not win in the end, but she wasn't ready to concede the fight yet. However, if she did lose, she'd rather it be to whoever the new bidder was than Tasha.

After a few more rounds, the dark-haired woman at table number two gave up once again, leaving Tasha as Tory's only competition.

"I now have twenty-two thousand; can I get twenty-four?" Courtney asked the crowd after acknowledging Tory's most recent bid.

Like everyone else in the room, Tory watched to see what her competition would do. This time, Tasha didn't come back with a higher bid, unlike earlier.

"Going once." From behind the podium, Courtney glanced around the crowd. "Going twice." Still, no further bids came. "Bidder number fifty-five is the winner of four romantic dates with Duncan Ferguson."

"Thank you for saving Duncan from Tasha," Alec commented as she stood up.

She wasn't big on being in the spotlight, but she had no choice tonight. And the sooner she got up on stage to collect

Duncan, the sooner she and Duncan could turn it over to someone else.

"Anytime."

DUNCAN HAD THOUGHT the night couldn't get much worse. Then he saw Tasha Marshall join the bidding war. Although he'd seen her at other events, he'd never spoken to the woman. But he knew her reputation. He couldn't think of anyone else who might be in attendance he'd rather be auctioned off to less. But either his luck was changing, or Tasha had decided she'd rather spend the money on someone else in the lineup, because he was leaving the stage with Tory Sherbrooke, not Tasha.

It'd been close to eighteen years, but Duncan remembered the first time he saw Tory. It'd been his third day of freshman year at Phillips Exeter, and he'd been on his way to English class. She'd been with a group of friends and passed him in the hallway. At the time, he hadn't known her name, what grade she was in, or that she and his roommate were cousins.

It hadn't mattered, though. From that second on, he'd had the biggest crush on her. For the rest of the week, he kept an eye out for her whenever he left his dorm room.

He'd finally learned her name and connection to his roommate six days later. He'd been eating dinner with Alec when Leah and Tory had stopped by their table. They stayed long enough to ask Alec how things were going and for his roommate to introduce Duncan to the two upperclassmen.

Although they didn't interact much, Duncan's crush remained firmly in place until Tory graduated two years later. These days, they occasionally found themselves at the same events, but he couldn't remember the last time they'd spoken.

So far, all the couples had returned to the audience after leaving the stage. Duncan expected they would do the same. But she paused at the bottom of the steps rather than lead him to where she'd been sitting.

"We can stay here if you want, but I thought it'd be nice to find a quieter place to catch up."

He had no desire to linger in the ballroom and watch Courtney auction off the remaining seven sacrifices. "Let's go somewhere else."

"It's nice out tonight, and since everyone is in here, the terrace is probably empty. I just need to get my purse."

Duncan didn't care what the weather was. He loved being outdoors, and some fresh air would be nice. "Lead the way."

While up on stage, he'd seen Alec and Gianna seated with Tory. Both were missing now.

"Did Gianna and Alec leave?" Duncan asked after he greeted the familiar faces sitting at the table. He hadn't seen his cousin in over a month and hoped to say hello at least.

One of Alec's cousins nodded. "According to Alec, they had someplace to be. But he said he'll call you soon," Callie said.

Yeah, right. It was more likely Alec had seen what he'd come for and gone back to his hotel room or wherever he and Gianna were spending the night.

"Duncan and I are going to find someplace quieter to talk." Tory slipped the strap of a purse so tiny he wondered what she could possibly keep in it over her shoulder.

"Will you be back?" Leah asked.

"Maybe."

They stopped so Tory could arrange payment and exited the lobby. Much like when he'd arrived, the area was empty except for two hotel employees.

"I'm sorry, the terrace is closed to guests this evening," a hotel employee informed them when they approached the glass doors leading outside.

The flickering candles and floral arrangements visible on the other side of the glass told a different story. The area was unavailable to most guests. Someone was using the terrace, and he could just make out the back of a man's head—one that, even from this distance, he recognized.

Rather than argue, Tory smiled and turned around. "It looks the opposite of closed to me," Tory said, her voice not much above a whisper as they walked away. "I'm pretty sure that's Alec and Gianna out there."

"When he came backstage to visit me, Alec told me he's proposing tonight. So my guess is he's doing it now."

"Well, it looks like he made it special."

Duncan agreed with her there. "Where to now? We can try the lounge downstairs. It might be a little more private than in there." He pointed toward the ballroom.

"Maybe." Her mouth formed a shadow of a frown. "I'm staying here, so we could go back to my suite."

He'd had women he didn't know invite him back to their hotel rooms, but he'd never accepted. Some lines he didn't cross. But Tory was more an acquaintance than a stranger, and while the lounge might be less crowded than the ballroom, it wouldn't be empty.

"Whatever you want. I'm staying here too, so we could also go back to my suite."

He could practically see the gears turning in Tory's head as he waited for an answer. "Let's go to my room. It's a Saturday night, so the lounge is probably crowded and noisy. I don't feel like shouting to be heard."

Duncan followed her into the elevator and watched as she pressed the button for the eighth floor. "I'm on that floor too. Suite 802."

"You're across the hall from me."

Two couples dressed for a night out joined them when the elevator stopped at the next floor, pausing any further conversation until they reached their destination.

"Make yourself comfortable." Tory left her purse on a table and headed into the small kitchenette.

Except for the pictures on the wall, Tory's suite was identical to his.

"Do you want anything to drink? After checking in this afternoon, I picked up some sparkling water and grapefruit juice."

He loved a glass of fresh grapefruit juice with breakfast. Or a combination of grapefruit juice and gin while sitting by the pool. He didn't want a glass of it at nine o'clock at night.

"Water is fine, thanks. How have you been?" Duncan sat in one of the two armchairs and waited for her to join him.

"Busy but good. I recently moved to Boston and started a new job." She handed him a glass and then sat on the sofa opposite him.

It would be a lot easier for them to go on their four dates with her living in the city, too. "Whereabouts in Boston?"

"Heritage on the Harbor Terrace. I bought Alec's condo last month."

He would've remembered if Alec had shared that information. "Alec didn't tell me he sold the condo to you, but welcome to the building. I'm on the fourth floor. I don't know if you've ever met Matt Sinclair? He's a friend of Alec's and me, but he lives in the building too."

"I don't think so, but since we're on the topic of my cousin, I got the impression tonight that he had something to do with you being part of the auction. Am I right?"

Duncan saw no reason to lie. "In a way. Alec, Matt, and I were playing poker one night back in June; I made a bet with Alec. Whoever lost had to be in the auction. When I came up with the idea, it seemed like there was no way I'd lose. But, clearly, I did, because I was on stage tonight, not him."

"Duncan, you can't just tell me you lost a bet and stop there. You need to share more details. And what did the winner walk away with?"

If she wanted to hear it, he'd share. "To win, Alec needed to work for my uncle's landscaping company for a month. It's where I worked every summer before I graduated from college.

It's not easy work. I didn't think your cousin would last even two days. But he did, and according to Gianna, he never complained, either. She was his boss and landlord."

"Ah, so that's how they met."

Duncan nodded as he took a drink.

"Since he won, what did Alec get?"

"The chance to see me up on stage tonight." There was no preventing the annoyance in his voice.

"That doesn't seem like much of a prize."

"Trust me, it was for your cousin. And if Alec had lost, I would've loved every minute of watching him suffer up there."

"I'll take your word for it."

She didn't sound convinced, but he'd told her the truth. "So they instructed us to plan the four dates in advance, but honestly, I only came up with something for the first one. If you'd rather do something else, that's okay with me. And then we can decide together what you want to do for the rest."

He'd come up with going to a wine tasting followed by dinner in the eleventh hour because he needed to give Courtney something to say while he was up on stage. But he wasn't married to the idea, and since she'd spent the money, it only seemed fair that Tory had a say in what they did together.

"I'm fine with whatever we do."

Tory was being far more agreeable than a lot of people he knew. "If you're free on Saturday, I'll call and make reservations tomorrow."

There was no set timetable for when all four dates had to take place, but the organizers expected the first to occur within two weeks of the auction. Since he had no plans this upcoming weekend, he saw no reason to postpone their first date.

Picking up her glass, she raised it toward her lips. Rather than take a drink, though, she set it back down and shifted her position. "Before you do that, I have a favor to ask. Although, maybe 'favor' isn't the right word. Anyway, what I'm about to ask is going to sound crazy, and I'll understand if you say no."

He couldn't imagine what kind of favor she'd need from him. However, she'd captured Duncan's attention, and he'd hear her out. "Ask away."

"The four dates aren't the real reason I bid on you tonight. A good friend is getting married soon, and I'm the maid of honor. Unfortunately, my ex is the groom's cousin and the best man. I ended things in August, but Grant still calls, and at my parents' dinner party last month, he never left my side."

"The guy just showed up at your parents' house?" Duncan knew a few people with the nerve to do that if it would benefit them in some way.

"No, my parents invited him. I know he's—"

"Hold on. Back up a minute." It was rude to interrupt, but curiosity got the better of him. "Your mom and dad invited your ex-boyfriend to their dinner party? Did they know you're no longer together?" What kind of parents would do that?

"Grant's parents and mine have been friends for years, so they often invite him to events. Anyway, I know Grant will do the same thing at the wedding. If I'm alone."

He already suspected what the favor was. Tory wanted him to be her plus-one for the wedding. Considering the circumstances, Duncan recognized why she didn't want to go solo, but spending twenty-four thousand dollars to ensure she had a wedding date was extreme. But it was her money; at least it had gone to a good cause.

"Hey, if you want the wedding to be one of our dates, that's fine." It saved him from having to come up with ideas.

"Not exactly, Duncan."

What the hell does that mean?

"Ivy and Preston are getting married in Puerto Rico. They have activities planned for the wedding party all week."

He'd had a friend do something similar when he got married. It had only been the three days leading up to the wedding, though, and in Aruba.

Tory clenched her hands together. "I was hoping you'd come with me and act like you're my boyfriend."

Yep, when Tory said it would sound crazy, she hadn't been lying.

"I know you donate your time and money to many charities."

How do you know that? As much as he wanted an answer to that question, he wouldn't interrupt her.

"So, in exchange for your help, I'll donate fifteen thousand to your favorite one and, of course, I'll pay for everything related to the trip."

Duncan donated to a handful of charities. However, he gave the most to an animal rescue organization in New Hampshire. His parents' neighbors had started it, and it was run entirely by volunteers. But unlike larger, nationwide animal rescues, it didn't have a multimillion-dollar annual budget. So a fifteen-thousand-dollar donation would help the organization a lot.

"I know it's an unusual request."

Unusual? More like desperate. He might not have as much experience with women as some men, but he knew when to keep his thoughts to himself. And this seemed like one of those times.

Perhaps his expression gave him away, though, because Tory added, "Believe me, I wouldn't be asking if I wasn't desperate."

At least we're on the same page there.

"You don't have to give me an answer tonight, Duncan. But I'll need one soon. If you come, I'll need to change my hotel reservation, because we'll need a suite with two bedrooms, and Ivy will need to add you to the guest list."

As CEO of the company, Duncan didn't need to get his vacation time approved by his boss, but that didn't mean he could disappear for a week whenever he wanted to, either.

"When is the wedding?" Duncan asked as he opened the calendar on his phone. Thankfully, only his family and closest friends knew he struggled with saying no when someone needed help. And if Tory had paid out all that money just to ask him and was willing to dish out more if he agreed, she had to be beyond desperate.

"November twenty-third, but Ivy and Preston expect the wedding party to be in Puerto Rico on the seventeenth."

He scrolled through the month of November. At the moment, the only things he had scheduled for that week were a haircut and dinner with his parents. He could easily reschedule both. But could he pull off pretending to be her boyfriend? Unlike Clay Bentley, bachelor number eight, he had zero acting experience.

If Duncan was smart, he'd play it safe and tell her he needed to think about it. But, instead, he'd follow his gut like he usually did. Right now, it was telling Duncan to help Tory out. "Yeah, sure, I'll go with you."

"Really?" Based on her expression and tone, a person would assume he'd just told her little green men lived on Mars and the moon was made of Swiss cheese. "Don't you want to think about it at least for the night? Whether you answer me now or in the morning doesn't matter."

Duncan shook his head. "It's a win for all of us. I get a vacation, you get to enjoy the wedding without your ex bothering you, and Southern New Hampshire Animal Rescue receives a nice donation they can really use."

"Um, I, um, I wasn't expecting an answer tonight. But thank you. I really appreciate it. Tomorrow I'll call and change my reservation at the hotel. I can see if there are any seats available on my flight too. Although, I guess we don't have to take the same one down as long as we arrive at the hotel together."

The last time he'd flown, his plane had taken off three hours late.

"It'll be better if we travel together. Flights get canceled and delayed all the time. And it'll look odd if I show up later than you." It might not happen, but he saw no reason to risk it either. "Do you have any plans for tomorrow?" he asked.

"Nothing except checking out and driving home. Why?"

"How about you come by for dinner tomorrow, then? If we're

going to pull this off, we need to get to know each other better. While you're there, you can fill me in on what we'll be doing that week, and we can also make my travel arrangements."

"Sounds like a great idea. What time?" she asked before taking a sip of juice.

He'd planned to sleep late in the morning and then have lunch with a friend and his wife who lived in the area. But, if Tory was going to join him for dinner, he'd need to visit the grocery store, because he didn't have much at home except for prepackaged meals that went in the microwave.

"Six?"

"Works for me," Tory answered with no hesitation.

"Is there anything you won't eat?"

His younger sister constantly changed what foods she would or wouldn't eat. About two years ago, she'd gone through a vegetarian stage before deciding it wasn't for her and becoming a pescatarian. Seven or eight months ago, she'd given that up and adopted a keto lifestyle. For all he knew, Tory might be a vegan. He didn't want to go through the work of making something she wouldn't eat.

"I'm not picky, but I can't eat mushrooms. I'm allergic to them."

Cooking for someone was so much easier when they weren't picky. "Okay, then I'll see you at six. I'm on the fourth floor in condo 4A."

FOUR

Thanks to his parents' efforts, Duncan could cook, repair anything in the house that might break, garden with the best of them, and sew. These days, cooking was the only skill from the list he used, and he only did it sometimes. But maybe he would start doing it more often.

He'd hated every second of food shopping. Duncan could handle a busy store and even toddlers throwing tantrums in the middle of the produce section, but he couldn't stand inconsiderate people. Today it'd been as if every jerk in Boston had decided to go food shopping. But once he returned home and started the prep work, enjoyment replaced his annoyance. It'd been so long since he prepared anything more complicated than pasta with store-bought sauce that he'd forgotten how much he enjoyed cooking.

Tonight he'd decided to prepare pesto chicken bruschetta. It was a dish he'd learned from his dad, who cooked as well as, if not better than, his mom—not that anyone in the family would ever say that. And like when Dad served it, Duncan made the pesto rather than bought it. He picked up dessert and the dinner rolls at the bakery because, although he cut lunch with his friends short, he returned to the city later than he'd hoped. Not to mention, unlike his sister, Duncan didn't enjoy baking.

His cell phone beeped as he read the meat thermometer he'd stuck into a chicken breast.

One hundred and sixty degrees. It was almost done, which was a good thing because he expected Tory in a few minutes.

Grabbing the device off the counter, it did not surprise him to find a text from his cousin. Considering Alec's announcement before walking away last night and then seeing the two of them on the hotel terrace, he'd been expecting one from Gianna all day.

Alec asked me to marry him last night.

He'd have to tell Tory he'd been correct.

And you said no, I hope. I'm not sure he's the type of person we want in the family.

He'd been born three months after Gianna, and he'd always considered her more a sister than a cousin. And like any sibling, he gave her a hard time whenever an occasion presented itself. This was undoubtedly one of those times.

It didn't take long for Gianna to reply.

Funny, your sister says the same thing about you all the time.

Although he didn't consciously set out to do it, he often found himself being the overprotective older brother. Rather than being thankful that he cared, Harper usually got pissed at him. Although, in his defense, Harper was eleven years younger than him, and sometimes he found it difficult to see her as anything but the four-year-old who used to walk around dressed as Dorothy from the Wizard of Oz while carrying their cat Peanut —because their dog was too large—in a basket.

She probably says worse.

A shrugging emoji appeared on his screen before Gianna's next text.

I said yes.

Congratulations. I'm happy for you.

He was happy for Alec too, and later he'd reach out to congratulate him.

When are you coming to the island again?

He'd hoped to get there sometime before Thanksgiving. But he wasn't sure that would happen now.

Not sure. I'll let you know.

No sooner did he type the message than his doorbell rang.

Got to go. Tory's at the door.

Duncan realized his mistake a second after he pressed send.

As in Alec's cousin? First date already?

Gianna wouldn't tell anyone if she knew the truth, but not only didn't he have the time, the situation was better explained over the phone. But, of course, that assumed Tory wouldn't mind if he told Gianna the truth.

Not exactly. I'll fill you in later.

Duncan didn't wait for a response before putting the phone in his back pocket and leaving the kitchen. He knew Gianna. She'd stew over his response but would wait until at least tomorrow before reaching out again. By then, he'd know if he could share the truth. And if Tory didn't want him to, he'd have enough time to come up with a plausible reason for why Tory stopped by tonight.

He'd thought she looked great at the fundraiser. Tonight, she looked terrific, dressed in dark jeans and an oversized green sweater that made her eyes look more green than the hazel they'd been last night.

"Hey, come on in," he said, taking a step back so she could enter.

"I stopped for wine and dessert on my way home this morning." She gestured toward the reusable bag and the bakery box she carried. "Since I didn't know what you were making, I got a chardonnay and a pinot noir. The dessert is from Ambrosia."

"Great minds think alike. I picked up dessert from there too."

"Thank my cousin. She suggested it when I asked what the best bakery in the area was. I've never had anything from there."

"You're in for a treat, then. They make the best cannoli and tiramisu on the east coast."

"There might be a piece or two of tiramisu in here. But, sorry, there are no cannoli."

"That's okay. I picked some up when I was out." After taking the box and bag from her, he walked toward the kitchen. "Can I get you anything to drink? I can open some wine or make you a cocktail."

He preferred beer to wine and always had some on hand, but he couldn't picture Tory enjoying a can of his favorite craft beer.

"Maybe with dinner. Some water is fine for now."

"Do you want sparking water or tap?" Tap water got boring, and he liked to mix it up sometimes.

"Sparkling," she answered, setting her purse on a stool at the island. Unlike the one she carried last night, this one looked large enough to hold a small child. "It smells amazing in here. I can't wait to taste whatever you made."

Usually, he drank straight from the bottle. Now, he poured the sparkling water into glasses and handed her one.

"Thank you. But I could've drunk it out of the bottle and saved you a dirty glass."

"If it'll make you feel better, I'll let you wash the glasses after dinner."

Tory scrunched up her nose. "And deprive you of all the fun? That doesn't seem very nice, especially since you cooked dinner and agreed to help me."

"That is very thoughtful of you." After checking the internal temperature of the chicken again, he removed it and put a piece on each plate.

"Thoughtful is my middle name. Do you need me to do anything?"

It should be "Beautiful." Once again, it was a thought better kept to himself.

Duncan placed a slice of fresh mozzarella on top of each

chicken breast and added the pesto and bruschetta. "If you want to put these on the table, I'll pour the wine."

"If this tastes even half as good as it looks, I might knock on your door every night for dinner," she said, accepting the plates and carrying them to the table.

"You're welcome to come by whenever you want, but I don't cook like this often."

"Me neither. I eat a lot of salads. They're quick and easy to make."

He was guilty of doing the same. Only, a snack consisting of chips or cookies often followed the salad.

"I said it last night, but thank you for agreeing to this crazy idea."

When he'd woken up this morning, he wondered if the previous evening had been a weird dream. Later, when he saw the picture of him and Tory together on the Providence Gazette's website, he'd briefly considered the possibility that the conversation in her suite was part of a practical joke Alec had asked Tory to help him with. But the situation was too crazy for even Alec to invent.

"I appreciate—"

The doorbell interrupted the rest of her statement.

"It's probably Matt," Duncan pushed back his chair. "He tends to just stop by these days. He's single again."

Matt had planned to attend last night's fundraiser. Unfortunately, his mom and grandmother threw a monkey wrench into things when they decided to spend a few days with him before flying down to Florida. And if there was one thing Matt couldn't do, it was say no to his mom and grandmother.

Duncan wished he'd checked his doorbell camera rather than open the door when he saw who stood on the other side. After Matt told him Lori Ann was once again living in the building, he'd expected a visit from her the next day. When it didn't happen and one week turned into two, he assumed she'd found a new BFF in the building.

It looked like he had been wrong.

"Hey, Lori Ann. Matt told me you were living in the building again. How have you been?"

"Crazy busy. That's why I didn't stop by and say hello sooner." Even though he hadn't invited her, she walked inside. "Are you cooking? Something smells amazing."

"Yes, Tory and I were just about to eat."

Frowning, Lori Ann glanced past his shoulder. But with Tory in the kitchen, all she saw was an empty living room. "Oh, I didn't think you would have company on a Sunday night. I'll let you get back to them." She held out the plastic container in her hands. "I'm made some chocolate chip cookies. I thought you might like some."

It would be rude not to accept the cookies. But, at the same time, if he took them, Lori Ann might start to bring him baked goods all the time, like before she moved.

"Thank you." He'd deal with one problem at a time. The most pressing one at the moment was getting Lori Ann to leave so he and Tory could get the details for their trip ironed out.

"Well, enjoy your dinner. Hopefully, we can catch up soon."

I'd rather not. "Have a nice night."

Duncan left the cookies on the counter before sitting back down. "Sorry about that. Lori Ann used to live in the unit next to me. She moved back into the building recently and wanted to say hello."

"I might have met her last week when I was down at the pool. Is she tall with long, blonde hair?"

Duncan nodded as he sliced his chicken. "That's her."

TORY CONSIDERED HERSELF A DECENT COOK, especially if she had a detailed recipe. However, the meal she had just finished was far better than anything she'd prepared in a long time. "That was delicious."

She'd already told Duncan that, but the meal had been so good it needed to be repeated.

"Can I get the recipe?" Whenever she had guests over for dinner, she struggled with what to make. If she served what they'd had tonight, not even her overly critical parents would complain.

"Sure. I'll write it down before you leave," Duncan said as he added the last of the dinner plates to the dishwasher. "Would you like some espresso or tea to go with dessert?"

"It should be against the law to serve anything but an espresso with tiramisu."

The smile Duncan flashed her had Tory wishing she'd opted for something lighter than a sweater tonight. "You and I are going to get along very well," he said.

Opening a cupboard, he took out three cans of espresso and set them on the counter. "Pick whichever one you want."

"I'll have the bold roast." She used the three brands at home and liked them all.

"That might be my favorite of the three." He put the other two cans away and got out some espresso cups. "By the way, I was right last night. Alec proposed to Gianna."

It looked like she'd be attending another family wedding soon. "I'll have to congratulate him later."

So far, the evening had been enjoyable, but she wasn't there to socialize or get new meal recipes. And with dinner behind them, now seemed like a good time to address the real reason he'd asked her over tonight. "I told Ivy I'm bringing a guest to the wedding."

"Was she okay with the late addition?"

"Bringing a fake boyfriend was her idea, so yeah, she didn't mind adding you."

"I thought my friends came up with crazy ideas."

Not only had she blindsided him last night with the request, but he'd answered without taking much time to think about it. He might be having second thoughts now but be too nice to say anything. If he was, she didn't blame him.

"You don't have to come. Trust me, I'd understand if you changed your mind, Duncan."

Duncan's fingers brushed against hers as he handed her a cup, sending tingles up her arm—something she hadn't experienced in a long time. "Ask your cousin. He'll tell you that once I agree to do something, I don't turn around and change my mind."

"I'll take your word for it." The world could use more people like that. "I changed my hotel reservation too. Our suite has two bedrooms, each with its own bathroom on the second level, and then on the first, we have a living room area, another bathroom, and a kitchenette. We also have two balconies."

"Sounds great. Where are we staying?"

"The Sherbrooke Caribe Beach Resort. The wedding is there too."

Perhaps the best resort on the island, Ivy and Preston hadn't even considered anywhere else when they decided to get married in Puerto Rico.

"I stayed there once several years ago while I was there for a conference." He took a sip from his cup as he put dessert plates on the kitchen island. "We'll be more comfortable if we bring dessert into the other room."

She didn't care where they ate dessert as long as she got some. Picking up the bakery boxes, she followed Duncan out of the kitchen. Heritage on the Harbor Terrace offered condos with several different floor plans, but the only difference between her living room and Duncan's was the furniture and the pictures on the walls. Even the view from the windows was the same.

"You can start eating without me. I'm going to grab my laptop from my office so we can look at flights," Duncan said, setting down plates and his espresso.

When tiramisu was around, other desserts didn't usually exist. But the eclairs she'd also bought looked delicious. So rather than pick between the two, she added half of each to her plate and grabbed a fork.

“I didn't know you bought eclairs too.” After taking the halves she'd left behind, Duncan added a cannoli to his plate as well and sat down next to her.

“They looked too good to pass up,” Tory answered before taking a bite. “Wow. They're good. I might have to go back and get more tomorrow.”

“You can't go wrong with anything from Ambrosia. Occasionally, I stop in at lunchtime and grab a sandwich.” After helping himself to a forkful of tiramisu, he opened his laptop and logged onto the internet. “What airline are you using?”

“Delta flight 1061 out of Boston. I checked earlier. There are still some first-class seats available.” Tory's cell phone beeped as she removed her credit card from the cardholder on it. “Use this for the ticket,” she said, handing him the card. Flipping the phone over, she groaned at the name on the screen.

Duncan's fingers paused over the keyboard, and he glanced over at her rather than type. “Everything okay?”

“Yeah, just a text from Grant. He's going to be in Boston later this week on business and wants to get together next weekend.” She wasn't sure what her plans were for the weekend, but seeing Grant wasn't among them. After sending Grant a generic message telling him she had plans and couldn't see him, she picked up her fork.

“That reminds me, I made our reservations for the winery on Saturday.”

Preoccupied with other things, she'd forgotten Duncan mentioned going on their first date on Saturday. “Sounds good.”

“I was thinking about this last night. So far, the only places I've found pictures of us together are the fundraiser's website and the Providence Gazette. It is possible some might appear somewhere else, though. Your friends might find it odd that you took someone you just met at a bachelor auction on vacation.” Duncan finished booking his flight as he spoke. “And if they don't find out about that, they might ask how we met. Should we come up with a story in case someone does?"

Between wondering if Duncan would tell her he'd changed his mind tonight and whether she'd lost her mind by asking him, Tory had thought about what she should say to her friends and, more importantly, Grant when she saw him later this month.

"Already well ahead of you."

She tried to keep things as close to the truth as possible while still making the story plausible, because while some people would accept that she'd asked a guy she'd just met to go away with her, others might not.

"If someone asks, we tell them we knew each other in high school, which is true. Then in September, when I was here looking at condos, we bumped into each other. Maybe we were both at Alec's house or something. Anyway, we spent a lot of time together the week and a half I was out here. And we decided to see where things went and did the long-distance thing until I came back last month. But because you'd already agreed to be in the auction, you couldn't back out, so I bid on you."

Nodding, Duncan reached for his espresso. "I'm impressed. When you said you were way ahead of me, you weren't kidding. I'm fine with using that story if anyone at the wedding asks. But let's not mention Alec. He wasn't in the city at all in September. Instead, how about we ran into each other the day you looked at your condo? It easily could've happened."

No one at the wedding would ever see Alec, so she didn't see why it mattered if they mentioned him. But if Duncan wanted to tweak their story, she'd go along with it. Since he'd been beyond cooperative so far, it was the least she could do.

"Works for me."

She still didn't know much about him, but tonight wasn't the only time they'd spend together. "Can you think of anything else we should talk about tonight?" she asked, struggling to hold back a yawn. Although she'd climbed into bed at a decent hour last night, she hadn't fallen asleep until well after two this morning because her stupid brain wouldn't stop.

Duncan cringed. Considering the topic, it wasn't an expression she wanted to see. "I slipped earlier and told Gianna you were at the door. Then, without thinking, I said no when she asked if we were going on our first date tonight."

Tory couldn't hold that against him. She was guilty of answering without thinking herself.

"Can I tell her what's really going on?"

Most people she knew wouldn't bother asking. Instead, they'd do whatever they wanted. It said a lot about Duncan's character that he'd asked her first. "If you want."

The chances of Duncan's cousin ever conversing with Grant or anyone else at the wedding was about as likely as the New England Rebels drafting Tory to play football.

"I'll let you know what I decide. I might tell her I invited you over so we could plan our other dates, which we still need to do."

"We don't need to do anything special for our dates." She'd meant to tell him that last night. "I think we'd get to know each other better by just spending time together like we did tonight."

They didn't need to know all of each other's secrets. However, if people were going to believe they were a couple, they needed to know more than that they both liked to drink espresso while eating tiramisu.

"There's no reason we can't do both."

She couldn't argue with him. And the more time they spent together before the wedding, the more comfortable they'd be with each other while in Puerto Rico. "I'm meeting a friend tomorrow night, but do you want to come by Tuesday around six for dinner?"

"I can't Tuesday, but I'm free Wednesday."

There was no stifling her yawn this time. "Wednesday at six works for me," Tory said, coming to her feet. "I'm sorry. If I sit here much longer, I will fall asleep."

"You really know how to boost a guy's ego."

"It's not you. I didn't—" Tory stopped when she spotted Duncan's grin. She was comfortable teasing and exchanging friendly insults with only a handful of people, individuals Tory knew well. But the way Duncan was smiling at her, she couldn't help it now. "On second thought, maybe the company is making me tired. I did feel fine when I got here."

"Wednesday, I'll try to be more entertaining. Maybe I'll even put on a show for you," he said as they reached the door.

"Now, I'm curious. What kind of show?"

"You'll have to wait and see."

FIVE

"DON'T BE SURPRISED IF YOU HEAR FROM GRANT. HE'S IN Boston this week." Ivy's voice came through Tory's earbuds as she prepared dinner on Wednesday night.

"Already did. On Sunday, he asked if we could get together this weekend." Tory added the chopped cucumbers to the salad and then reached for the tomatoes. "I told him I had plans."

"I wish he'd meet someone already."

"You and me both. But hopefully when he sees me with Duncan in Puerto Rico, he'll accept there is no chance of us getting back together and move on."

"Have you and Duncan gone on your first date yet?"

"No, we're going on Saturday, but last Sunday, he cooked us dinner. And he's coming by tonight. If we're going to pull this off at the wedding, we need to get to know each other."

"Wait a minute. He cooked dinner for you, and you didn't tell me. Was it any good?"

"It was delicious. Even my parents would've enjoyed it, and you know how picky they are." Tory placed the salad down on the table and then turned off the buzzing oven timer.

"Maybe you should see if he's interested in an actual relationship. I don't think there are too many men around that can cook a meal good enough for them."

She couldn't argue with Ivy there. They'd been known to complain at the best five-star restaurants in Beverly Hills.

"Hey, I need to let you go. Preston just walked in, and we're heading over to his parents' house. It's his mom's birthday."

Before Tory could respond, the doorbell rang. "Good timing. Duncan's at the door anyway."

At least she assumed it was him. She wasn't expecting anyone else tonight. If Grant knew her address, she'd worry it was him since he was in town, but he didn't have that. Thank goodness. "Have fun and say hello to Preston for me."

"Will do."

When she opened the door a moment later, Tory's eyes immediately zeroed in on the black guitar case slung over Duncan's right shoulder. She'd heard of people bringing dessert or maybe flowers when they visited someone. She'd never heard of anyone bringing a guitar with them.

"You brought a guitar with you?" The evidence was right in front of her, so it was a silly question, but she asked it anyway.

"The other night I promised you a show when I came over so that I didn't put you to sleep again." The warmth of his smile echoed in his voice. "I couldn't find my old magic set, so I brought my guitar instead."

She'd forgotten all about the comment until now. "I guess it's a good thing you play the guitar and not the piano. You would've had a difficult time getting one up here on your own."

"Oh, I play that too. It was the first instrument I learned. But I don't own one. I also play the saxophone, but it's in my parents' basement. Or it used to be. They might have gotten rid of it by now."

"I'm impressed. I gave up piano lessons after a year and never tried anything else." She hadn't wanted to take them in the first place. Instead, she'd had her heart set on learning to play the drums after seeing an old clip of Led Zeppelin in concert.

"Playing music isn't for everyone," Duncan said, following her into the kitchen.

"For me, it was more a matter of it not being the instrument I wanted to learn."

"What did you want to play?"

"The drums. Mom had other ideas. She didn't think it was an instrument a girl should be playing. But she let my brother try it."

"It's never too late to learn."

Tory shrugged. "True, but it would be a little embarrassing to take lessons now." She envisioned herself in a waiting room surrounded by ten-year-old children and their parents. She didn't want to play the drums that badly.

"If you ever change your mind, I have a friend who could teach you. He'll even come to your house and give lessons if you don't want to go to his studio." While she returned to the counter, Duncan stopped near the kitchen island. "Do you need any help?"

"Nope, everything is just about ready. Can I get you something to drink?"

"Whatever you're having is fine."

"So, what style of music are you going to play for me tonight?" Tory asked as she poured them each a glass of iced tea. A lot of people considered it more a summer beverage, but she drank it year-round. The same was true of lemonade and hot chocolate. She would not let the temperature dictate what she drank.

"You're going to have to wait and see."

"More like hear," she said, handing him a glass. "Have a seat." She gestured toward the table before putting the iced tea away.

Much like on Sunday night, something about Duncan made her comfortable enough to joke with him in a way she couldn't usually do with people until she got to know them well.

"That sounds like something my sister would say."

"I like her already."

Before joining him at the table, Tory grabbed the plate of pork chops and the two notebooks she'd left on the counter earlier. Considering what he served on Sunday, she'd planned to prepare a slightly more elaborate meal tonight, but she'd got caught up on a project she was working on and lost track of time.

"Dinner isn't as exciting as the one you made," she said, sitting down across from him.

"It looks good to me. And if I wasn't here, I would've grabbed takeout on the way home or had something delivered. It was one of those days."

"I had that kind of day yesterday." It was just one of the reasons she had trouble sleeping. Rather than stare at the ceiling, she'd started her own version of twenty questions. Although in this case, it was closer to seventy-five questions. "Last night, my dinner consisted of raisin bran cereal and peanut butter toast."

Duncan accepted the salad bowl she held toward him. "Believe me, I've had worse dinners than that."

Once or twice she'd devoured a pint of ice cream for dinner, but she wasn't about to admit that to him.

"Last night, I started a list of things we would most likely know about each other if we'd been friends in school and together since September." Making lists was kind of her thing. And she needed to write them on paper. No neatly typed lists on the computer for her.

Tory waited until he finished filling his salad plate before holding out one of the two notebooks she'd carried over. "I thought we could work on them tonight."

Duncan's eyebrows rose slightly, but he accepted the notebook. He scanned the first page in silence as he poured dressing over his salad.

"If there is anything you can think of that I missed, we'll add it." Following her dinner companion's lead, she poured her favorite dressing over her salad and waited for him to comment.

Duncan glanced at her as he stabbed a tomato and then flipped to the second page. His expression didn't give away his thoughts as he kept reading.

"A get-to-know-you cheat sheet wouldn't have occurred to me," Duncan finally said as he turned to the third page. "How long did you spend on this?"

She shrugged while cutting her pork chop. "I'm not really sure. My brain refused to turn off when I went to bed, so I worked on it until I fell asleep." She'd still been upright in bed when she woke up this morning, and both notebooks had been in her lap, but he didn't need that much detail. "Then a few more things came to me while I cooked dinner."

"The only question not in here is what my shoe size is." Duncan moved the notebook aside and reached for his knife. "I wear a size twelve, by the way."

Once again, he flashed her a smile that had her wondering why he was still single. The guy was handsome, successful, and had not only a great personality but a good sense of humor. What more could a woman want in a man?

"Good to know, but I'm not sure that'll come up in a conversation over a round of drinks."

"You never know. People ask weird questions when they've had one too many. Or while we're there, all the women might decide to go shoe shopping for their significant others. You don't want to be the only who doesn't know what size to buy. Talk about embarrassing."

"In that case, I wear a seven and half in heels. You know, just in case Preston drags all the guys into a Gucci store. If you end up in an Adidas store instead, my sneakers are an eight. If it's a Nike store, don't bother buying me anything. Their sneakers don't fit me right no matter what size I buy."

"Since you didn't give me a pen, I'll make a mental note to add all that later." A hint of humor laced his voice, and Tory couldn't help but smile.

She realized the lists were a little silly but wanted to be

prepared for any questions that might pop up. That didn't mean she was opposed to poking a little fun at the questions.

"Do you think we should add our blood types?"

About to scoop up some scalloped potatoes, Duncan paused. "That one I think we can safely skip. Most people don't even know their own blood type."

He had a point. She only knew hers because she donated blood four times a year.

"All joking aside, the lists aren't a bad idea. I just wasn't expecting something like them. If you want to start on the questions now, we can." He ate the potatoes before getting another forkful.

The sooner they started, the sooner they'd be done and Duncan could go home. But she wasn't in any rush to see him leave. She was enjoying his company too much. And like he'd stated Saturday night, if they were going to convince everyone in Puerto Rico they were a couple, they needed to get to know each other. Lists would help, but like the internet articles, they were a poor substitute for spending time together.

"If you're in a rush, we can work on the questions while we eat. Otherwise, let's do it after," she answered.

"No rush at all."

MUCH LIKE DUNCAN had done when he cooked for them, Tory refused his help after dinner. So, while she took care of the dishes and made them coffee, he performed a few songs for her. He'd never land himself a record contract, but he was a better-than-average guitar player, and he had a decent voice.

"I thought I was only getting an instrumental concert. Unlike me, you won't embarrass yourself on karaoke night." Tory joined him in the living room and put the tray she'd carried in on the coffee table beside the notebooks he'd brought in earlier.

He'd performed karaoke a handful of times but not in a

while. "Is that something your friend has planned for the wedding party?"

Tory had mentioned the bride had a week of activities lined up, but she hadn't given him specifics. In all fairness, he hadn't asked either. Maybe he should have, though. Although at this point, it didn't really matter. He'd already agreed to go with Tory, and no matter what she said, he wouldn't back out.

"Yep. I tried to talk her out of it, but she wouldn't budge. Ivy and Preston love karaoke. They regularly go out on weekends to places that have it. Unfortunately for anyone with ears, they're both tone deaf."

"Karaoke is all about having fun, not sounding good."

"Tell that to the people whose hearing Preston has destroyed over the years."

He couldn't help but laugh at her comment. "I haven't heard many people who can sing well get up and perform karaoke."

"I'm nowhere near as good as you, but I at least won't cause any dogs to howl in pain. The same cannot be said for my friends. I suggest you consider bringing earplugs for when Ivy and Preston get up on stage."

"Thanks for the warning. I'll be sure to pick up a pair."

"How long have you been playing the guitar? You're really good," Tory asked, changing the subject.

He tried to remember when he'd started as he returned his guitar to its case. "About twenty years or so. I did piano lessons first, and after a couple of years, I added the guitar."

"You did them at the same time?"

"Yeah, and then in sixth grade, I joined the school band and played the saxophone." Although the room offered numerous spots to sit, he joined her on the sofa. "You might want to write that down in your notes. You never know when you might need to know that."

It had surprised him when he opened the notebook and saw line after line of neatly written questions. But he couldn't argue with the logic behind them. They knew little about each other, which would be fine if they wanted people to believe they'd started dating after the auction. It wouldn't fly if they were going to convince people they'd known each other since high school and had been together for well over a month. A list like the one Tory complied ensured they didn't overlook anything important.

A dimple appeared in her right cheek when she smiled. "Already planned too." Picking up both notebooks, she handed him the zebra-striped one and kept the one with a cheetah pattern for herself.

"You like animal prints, don't you?"

"What gave it away?" Her smile grew wider as she held out a pen, and he couldn't help but smile himself.

"Lucky guess."

They zipped through the first few questions, which covered middle names, birthdays, and parents' names. The next question related to siblings.

"I know you have at least one sister because you mentioned her earlier. Is she younger or older than you?" Tory asked, pen poised over the paper.

"Harper is eleven years younger."

"Yikes, that's just a little bit of an age gap. Do you have any other siblings?"

"Technically, no, but Gianna is more like a sister to me than a cousin. She was born a few months before me, and she's an only child. Before my family moved off Sanborn Island, we did everything together. And every summer until I graduated from college, I'd stay with Gianna's family and worked for my uncle Corey's landscaping business. The same one Alec worked for this year."

"Leah and I are like that. But we didn't get really close until we roomed together at Phillips," Tory said, writing the information in her notebook.

"How many siblings do you have?" Alec had invited him to many Sherbrooke events since they'd first become friends, and he'd met too many family members to know how they were all related to each other.

"Two brothers. Adam is eighteen months older, and the one Mom let take drum lessons. Tyler is two years younger."

Duncan knew he wouldn't forget the names, but he wrote them down anyway because it seemed like the thing to do. "Are the three of you close?"

Some of his friends couldn't stand their siblings. Matt was a perfect example of that. Although Matt got along with his sister, he hadn't spoken to his brother in two years. Others, like Alec, were a tight-knit group. In fact, he'd always envied the relationship Alec had with his brothers and sister. While Duncan would do anything for Harper, the eleven-year age gap between them made it hard to have a relationship similar to the one Alec had with his siblings.

When she answered, he couldn't decipher Tory's expression. "I'm closer to Adam than Tyler."

If Tyler was two years younger than Tory, he was Duncan's age. "Tyler didn't go to school with us." The only Sherbrooke in his graduating class had been Alec.

Tory shook her head. "Nope. He was supposed to go to Phillips and share a room with Alec. But Tyler wanted to attend Cate with a friend. And whatever Tyler wants, Tyler gets."

Duncan was glad Tyler had gone somewhere else, because if he hadn't, Duncan might have found himself living with one of the many jerks at the school. And there had been plenty of them who didn't want to associate with someone there on a full-academic scholarship like Duncan. "I've never heard of Cate."

"It's in California and much smaller than Phillips. Tyler never said it, but I think a big part of the reason he wanted to go there was because he didn't want to be so far away from our parents. I love him, but he's always been a bit of momma's boy. He went to college in California too."

He knew the type. "Next question. Where did you grow up?"

"For the most part, Healdsburg, California, but I spent a lot of time at my parents' house in Palo Alto too," Tory answered.

Duncan was familiar with Palo Alto. Stanford University, which he'd toured and considered attending, was located there. "I've never heard of Healdsburg. Where's it located?"

"It's not far from Sonoma."

Wine country was on his lists of places he wanted to visit. Somehow, he just hadn't gotten around to it yet.

"What about you?" Tory asked once again, her pen poised over her notebook.

"I lived on Sanborn Island until I was eleven. Then we moved to Windham." Now he understood why his parents had accepted better-paying jobs and made the move, but he hadn't at the time. He'd just known his parents were making him move away from his friends and family.

Fifteen minutes later, only the last question on the first page didn't have an answer next to it. They would've covered that one and some on the second if they hadn't gone off topic more than once.

"After this question, I'm going to head home. I still have some work to do tonight." If he stayed here much longer, he'd end up falling asleep while sitting at his desk. It had happened before, and he didn't want to start his day tomorrow with a sore neck.

"You won't get an argument from me." Tory yawned, causing Duncan to do the same.

Uncertain of his answer, Duncan read the last question first to buy himself more time. "Favorite television show?"

Tory didn't even need time to think before answering. "I love the old black-and-white shows from the '50s and early '60s. The comedies and the westerns are probably my favorite, but I'll watch any of them."

He'd expected something more along the lines of the reality shows his sister loved to watch. He didn't think there was an episode of *America's Got Talent* or *Dancing With the Stars* that

Harper hadn't seen. And whatever you do, don't ask her about *Project Runway*.

"There are a few old black-and-white shows I like, but none of them are westerns."

He could handle an episode of *I Love Lucy*, *Lost In Space*, or even *The Andy Griffith* Show. But thanks to his grandmother, he'd seen enough episodes of *Bonanza* and *Gunsmoke* to last him a lifetime.

"I'm not sure we can be friends if you don't like old westerns." The dimple in her cheek appeared again, and much like when she'd yawned, he couldn't help but smile too. "Since old westerns are out, what is your favorite show?"

"You know, I don't think I have one. I don't watch a lot of TV, and when I do it's usually a baseball game or a historical documentary."

"History buff too?" Tory asked once again, taking them off topic.

"Guilty."

She simultaneously yawned and closed her notebook. "In that case, I can look past your other shortcomings."

"That's a relief."

SIX

"EXCEPT FOR WHEN I WAS AT PHILLIPS, I HAVEN'T SPENT MUCH time in New Hampshire. I don't think I've ever been to this part of the state."

Duncan slowed down as they approached the flashing yellow light. "It's the opposite for me. I spent most of my life in New Hampshire. And if the commute into Boston wasn't so horrible, I'd live here now."

"Yeah, the commute is why I didn't look for a place outside the city. I can work from home some days, but not all the time. And I didn't want to deal with the traffic when I have to go into the office."

Her comment reminded him of the mental note he'd made last night on his way home. "Where—"

"If—" Tory started at the same time.

"You first." Duncan pulled over when he saw a police cruiser barreling down the road behind him with its lights flashing. No sooner did it pass him than a fire truck flew by his car.

"If getting into Boston wasn't an issue, where would you live?"

Tory's question required no thought. "My first choice would be Sanborn Island. And if I only needed to go into the office occasionally like Alec or had a transporter handy, I'd live there year-round. My second choice would be somewhere in the White Mountains area of the state. I'm not sure exactly which town. There are a lot of nice ones up there."

"I've never been to Sanborn. And I'm not sure I've traveled to the White Mountains area. It's possible we competed against schools there when I ran track, but I don't remember."

He wasn't in the habit of inviting women he'd just met to spend the night at his house. But, then again, he hadn't just met Tory, and this wasn't a normal situation. "You have to visit the island at least once in the off-season. I love it there anytime, but crowds make truly enjoying it difficult during the summer. If you want, we can ride the ferry over on Saturday morning. It leaves out of Portsmouth, which is roughly an hour from Boston, depending on traffic. Then we can take the last ferry back or spend the night at my house there."

He'd purchased the home at the end of August but had spent little time there—something he hoped to do now that tourist season had ended.

"A trip over on Saturday sounds nice. But let me get back to you. Fingers crossed, I'll get all my projects wrapped up by Friday. But if I don't, I'll need to work next weekend. I want nothing hanging over my head while I'm in Puerto Rico, and I'm not bringing work with me."

"Sounds good. Just let me know." He'd spent the last two nights working until midnight for the same reason.

"Okay, your turn. What were you going to ask me before I interrupted you?" Tory asked.

"Where do you work?"

Many, but not all, of the Sherbrookes worked for the family's hotel chain or its largest charitable organization, the Helping Hands Foundation. He'd already ruled out the foundation. She would've moved to Providence, not Boston, if she worked for it.

"That is something you should know, isn't it?" Tory

answered. "I'm the marketing director for *Boston Home, Life, and Style Magazine*."

After stopping at the intersection, Duncan turned left onto Vineyard Lane. "Never heard of it." But, then again, it didn't sound like a magazine that would interest him or any of his friends, either.

"It's been around for eight years. I'm good friends with the cofounder's daughter. Sienna works there too, and she knew I was looking for a change. So when the position opened, Sienna suggested I apply."

"What did you do before you went to work at the magazine?" Duncan asked as he turned into Primrose Winery and Restaurant's main parking lot.

"I worked as the assistant marketing director at Desjardin Winery."

If he'd known she'd worked for a winery, he would've taken her somewhere else today. "A winery is probably the last place you want to spend your day then. I can call and cancel our reservations."

"We're already here, and I enjoy wine tastings. Besides, when I worked at Desjardin, I spent my days in the office, and the only wine I saw was in pictures. Although the job would've been much more interesting if we'd had samples on hand."

"I imagine it would've been."

He wouldn't argue with her if she was okay with their plans, especially since he didn't have any other ideas for the day.

Although he'd never seen the place empty, today looked busier than usual. Duncan was about to look for a place in the lot by the apple orchard when he saw a car backing out.

"This looks like a popular place," Tory commented as he pulled into the spot and shifted the car into park. "I've never heard of this winery. How did you find it?"

"When we left Sanborn, we moved to a town not far from here. My parents still live there. They're the ones that told me about it. The restaurant here is one of their favorites, and I've been here a few times with them and my sister."

He intended to open the car door for her, but Tory was already closing it by the time he reached the other side. "Looks like this was a farm at one time," she said, adjusting the straps of her purse. Unlike earlier in the week, this one wasn't large enough to double as a body bag. But he still couldn't imagine what she carried around that she needed such a purse.

Based on the old photos hanging inside the winery and the restaurant next door, Primrose Winery and Restaurant occupied the land where a large farm with multiple buildings had once been. According to its website, the current owners purchased the property twenty-five years ago. Before purchasing it, the husband-and-wife team had been experimenting with making wine using grapes and other fruits at their home. Once they'd perfected their technique, they purchased the old farm and started producing on a larger scale. Now the largest of the three original structures served as a tasting room and winery. The farmhouse operated as a restaurant, and customers could rent the small barn off to the left for private events such as weddings and retirement parties. He'd never counted to verify it, but the website claimed Primrose produced thirty different wines today.

Ten of them were made from grapes, while the others were made from fruits grown either on the property or in the area.

"I love when people repurpose old buildings. I wish more people would do that instead of tearing them down."

He'd had similar thoughts in the past. "Me too, but older buildings are a lot of work. I spent ten years living in an old house. My dad was always fixing something. He still is. Last year, he remodeled an upstairs bathroom. It was frozen in the 1930s. For him, it's kind of a hobby, and he enjoys it. Most people, though, don't have the time, skill, or money to maintain an older home."

"True, but it's still unfortunate. Some of them have unique details that aren't found in houses today."

Although the owners had replaced the old barn doors with large glass ones, the original wooden planks still covered the floor, and the large beams supporting the structure remained exposed. A bar spanned the left wall, and tables that could accommodate either four or six customers occupied the center of the building. On the right, a staircase led to a private room upstairs that customers could reserve for small gatherings. And at the far end of the building, another set of glass doors led to the outside patio. Customers occupied almost all the seats while others waited at the bar for their orders.

“Good afternoon. We're unable to accept any more walk-ins at this time. Do you have a reservation?” the employee at the hostess station asked.

He'd been enough times to know that, while reservations weren't required, the winery highly recommended them. And if a person didn't have one, there was a chance they'd be turned away, especially on the weekends.

“We do. It should be under Ferguson.”

Next to him, Tory moved closer so that a group of women could walk past them, and her hand brushed against his. Instantly, the muscles in his arm clenched as an electric jolt shot across his skin. If his body reacted like that to such a brief touch, he'd probably go into cardiac arrest if something less innocent happened between them.

No, not probably. Would.

What they'd shared on stage the previous weekend barely qualified as a kiss, yet it had sent his pulse to a place it'd never been.

The employee typed the name into her tablet and then handed him a pager. “You're welcome to wait in here or outside. I'll page you when your table is ready.”

“Do you want to wait in here or outside?” Duncan asked, moving away so the group behind them could check in.

“It's too nice to wait inside.”

“I was thinking the same thing.”

The grounds at the winery always tastefully reflected the season. Today, colorful mums, pumpkins, and bales of hay decorated the area. Several couples were taking advantage of the picturesque fall backdrop and were taking photos.

"Fall might be my favorite season," Duncan said, stopping far enough away from the cornstalks so that he didn't end up in anyone's picture. "What about you? What's your favorite?"

"I'm not sure I have one. But there's something I like about all of them."

"Not me. There's nothing I like about the spring. I always think winter is over, and soon we're going to have some warmer days. Instead, it always ends up being cold and rainy. Even in May, we sometimes get freezing rainstorms." Duncan noticed his former classmate and neighbor walking toward them even before Lou called out.

"Hey, Duncan. I thought that was you over here. It's been a while. How have you been?" Lou Barton asked as he and a woman Duncan didn't know stopped near them.

Lou had lived two houses down from him growing up, and they'd gone to school together until Duncan left for high school. About a year ago, Duncan bumped into Lou while visiting his parents. At the time, Lou had recently moved back to New Hampshire and accepted a position in Concord. And until the contractor finished renovating the house he'd purchased, Lou was living with his parents.

"I've been busy but otherwise okay. What about you?"

Well, if he had to run into someone he knew here, Duncan would rather it be Lou Barton than his parents or, worse, his sister. Mom wouldn't do it with Tory standing there, but later she'd call, subtly inquiring about their relationship. His sister would do the same—only she wouldn't be subtle. The word subtle wasn't in Harper's vocabulary. He couldn't tell Mom or Harper the truth, and he certainly didn't want to lie to them.

"Couldn't be better," Lou said before introducing them to his fiancée, Noelle.

"It's great to meet you." He needed to play his role at some point, and now seemed as good a time as any to try it. "This is my girlfriend, Tory," he said, resting an arm across her shoulders. "Lou and I used to be neighbors. His parents live in the gray house with the black shutters." Lou and his fiancée didn't know Tory had never visited Mom and Dad.

Without missing a beat, Tory leaned into him, and her arm snaked around his waist. The feel of her body against his had him instantly questioning his decision to touch her. Every nerve ending in his body switched off, except for those in contact with Tory. Those all fired at once, and he almost expected to see fire leaping from his clothes.

"You look so familiar. But I don't know from where," Noelle said.

If their proximity affected Tory the way it did him, she gave no indication. "I only moved to the East Coast recently."

"What do you say we ask to be seated together? Then we can catch up," Lou said.

Damn it. He hated when people put him on the spot like that.

Before he could answer, Tory squeezed his side. "We'd love to join you."

The hostess had no problem accommodating their request, and a few minutes later, she led them to a table.

"Practice makes perfect," Tory whispered in his ear as they followed Lou and Noelle.

THE RATIONAL PORTION of Tory's brain recognized the purpose of their outing today was to fulfill the terms of the auction and to further their acquaintance so they could pull off their charade. But, unfortunately, that part hadn't stopped her emotional half from looking forward to seeing Duncan for the past two days. She'd even considered calling him last night and asking him if he wanted to come over. Twice she'd pulled up his number on her phone. Both times, though, she'd reminded herself he'd agreed to play a role, not become her best friend and dinner companion. He might renege on their agreement if she demanded too much of his time, leaving her to face Grant alone. Under no circumstance did she want to find herself in that situation.

Picking up her menu, Tory scanned the various wines listed. "Does anyone have any recommendations?" Even if she ruled out the traditional varieties of wine, it left her with a lot of options. She'd prefer to avoid ordering something that wasn't good.

"I tried the Blueberry Merlot the last time I was here. It was delicious. My mom likes the Primrose Blush," Duncan replied. "She always buys a few bottles for the house when she comes."

"You definitely want to try the Primrose Blush," Noelle added. "It's my favorite. They make it from apples, pears, and elderberries. It's like no other wine I've ever had."

Each flight consisted of four two-ounce samples. Unfortunately, there were more than four on the menu Tory wanted to try, and she might never return here again. "If we each pick out different ones and share, we'll be able to try more, Duncan."

"That's what Lou and I are doing," Noelle answered before Duncan could agree or disagree. "We did the same thing the last time we came too."

"Sure, I'm fine with that. Why don't you pick the ones you want first, and then I'll choose?"

In the end, Tory opted for four wines not made from grapes, including the Primrose Blush, while Duncan's flight consisted of four traditional styles.

"Where did you live before you moved here?" Noelle asked as their server placed water glasses and appetizer plates on the table.

"California."

Noelle handed an appetizer plate to Lou before taking one for herself. "I lived outside of Sacramento until I was sixteen. I'd move back in a heartbeat. Whereabouts did you live?"

"Sonoma."

"And you moved here? Why?" Noelle's voice went up an octave. "That area is one of my favorite places to visit. Lou and I considered going there on our honeymoon. But we decided on Hawaii since we're getting married in February, and neither of us has ever been there."

It was a fair question. Northern California was a beautiful area, and many people enjoyed visiting. "I was ready for a change."

Across the table, Noelle slipped her hand over Lou's. Although holding hands was a minor thing, she and Duncan would need to do it while in Puerto Rico. So now seemed like as good a time as any to start.

Before she second-guessed herself, she covered Duncan's hand with hers and entwined their fingers. "A friend told me about an open position in Boston, and I applied."

"I cannot wait to get out of the city. Four years of commuting in and out is more than enough. Next month, I start working out of the company's Londonderry office."

"I bought a condo in Duncan's building for that exact reason."

"Is that how you two met?" Lou asked before taking a sip of water. Although he'd been the one to suggest sitting together so he and Duncan could catch up, his fiancée had done most of the talking so far.

"Actually, Tory and I went to high school together," Duncan answered, as the employee set down the charcuterie board they'd ordered. Once she walked away, he shared the story they'd agreed upon earlier in the week.

At least to her, it sounded convincing. And nothing in Lou or Noelle's expression suggested they didn't believe it.

Maybe they would pull this off.

AFTER LEAVING THE WINERY, they'd headed back into the city for a romantic dinner at what she suspected was Boston's best Italian restaurant. The emphasis there was on the word "romantic."

When they had arrived, an employee escorted them to a private room upstairs, away from the main dining area and bar, where Tory had found a dozen long-stemmed red roses waiting for her. Throughout the meal, soft music had played through the speakers, just loud enough for them to hear but not interrupt a conversation, while light from the various candles around the room bounced off the Tuscan limestone lining the walls. After dinner, they went to Duncan's favorite café for dessert and coffee before heading home.

"The last time I had Italian food that good, I was in Italy." Tory pressed the button for the elevator. "I'm going to have to go back there."

"Emilia is by far my favorite restaurant in Boston. I wish they delivered."

Between their visit to the winery and then dinner, they'd spent a decent part of the day together. Despite that, she wasn't ready to see their time together end. That didn't mean Duncan shared her feelings. He might be counting down the minutes until they went their separate ways for the night.

"It's only eight. Do you want to come over?" When the elevator doors opened, Tory stepped inside and pressed the button for her floor. "We could finish going through those questions or watch something on TV." Her finger hovered near the button for Duncan's floor.

"I was going to ask you the same thing. But let's save the questions for another night. I don't feel like going through them, and we still have time."

She was okay with that. "Which one would you rather go to, your place or mine?"

"Doesn't matter to me."

If Duncan didn't care, they'd go to her place. She'd been

looking forward to kicking off her shoes for over an hour, and she couldn't do that at his place.

"Is there anything specific you feel like watching?" Tory grabbed the remote off an end table and switched on the flat-screen television mounted to the wall after they entered her entertainment room.

"I'm open to suggestions," he said, making himself at home in her favorite spot on the sofa. Although you could see the television from anywhere in the room, she didn't have to sit at an angle to see the screen or worry about the glare from the sun when she sat in that corner of the sofa. Plus, the end table was right next to it, so she had a place to put a drink or snack while watching a movie.

Mom had a lot of beliefs when it came to what her daughter should and shouldn't do. Some Tory agreed with, and others she didn't. However, never intentionally being rude was one they both agreed on. And asking a guest to move because he was sitting in her preferred spot to watch television would be not only rude but downright childish.

"I know how much you love *Gunsmoke*, but unfortunately, I don't own the series," she said, logging into her library.

Duncan's shoulders drooped, and he placed a hand over his chest. "I don't know what to say. I'm heartbroken. I don't know if I'll ever recover."

He might not be an actor, but damn, he was good. If she hadn't known how he really felt about the old westerns, she'd think he was distraught.

"I'll work on buying it so I have it the next time you come over. Promise."

"Well, since that's out for tonight, what are my options?" he asked.

She couldn't have her favorite spot on the sofa, so she sat in the next best, the one next to Duncan. "Stop me if you see something you want to watch," she said, scrolling through the television series she owned. She'd switch over to her movie collection if they saw nothing there.

"You have the original *Lost In Space*?" he asked when she reached the 1960s sci-fi series. "I was something like eleven or twelve when I watched that. My aunt and uncle took Gianna, CJ, and me skiing for school vacation. The place they rented had a closet full of old VHS tapes. So Gianna, CJ, and I would watch a few episodes every night when we got back from skiing. But we didn't get through all of them."

She'd stumbled upon reruns of the old sci-fi show sometime in her teens. And when she found it again for sale last year, she'd purchased it. "I've got all three seasons. Although the second half of season three is not very good."

Actually, she forced herself to watch them because she wanted to see how the series ended. But, unfortunately, there was no proper ending to show.

"Why don't we watch that," Duncan said.

"Do you want to start with the original pilot or the actual first episode?" Tory opened the folder containing the three seasons.

"I didn't know there was a difference, so you pick."

Tory scrolled down to the official first episodes and pressed play. "We'll skip the original pilot. It's not a bad episode, but they use segments of it in later ones."

"Have you seen the new version? It's not bad," Duncan said as the show's theme song started.

She'd binge-watched each season as they came out. "Yeah, I watched it. Overall, I liked it, but there were a few changes they made I didn't love. Like how they wrote the parents' relationship for the first half of season one." The parents had been happily married in the original series, but it had been the opposite for about the first half of season one in the newer version.

"That didn't bother me. I didn't care for the way they changed Dr. Smith's character."

"You didn't like they made the character a woman?"

"It wasn't that." Duncan pulled his beeping cell phone from his pocket as he spoke. "Not again," he muttered.

"Is something wrong?" She paused the television just as the opening credits finished.

Duncan scowled and set his phone down. "Lori Ann is at my door."

She'd seen the woman twice this week at the pool. Both times, Lori Ann had been friendly.

"And that's a bad thing? I got the impression the two of you were friends," she said. "She brought you home-baked cookies last weekend when I was there." Not that she baked cookies often, but she'd only give them to friends if she did.

After taking in a deep breath, Duncan exhaled. "I don't know what you'd call us, but it's not friends."

"Is she an ex-girlfriend?" On Sunday, he'd told her Lori Ann used to live next door to him. That didn't mean she couldn't also be an ex-girlfriend. And if Lori Ann were, she wouldn't be the first person to want to rekindle a relationship that ended.

"No, we never went out. When we were neighbors, I made the mistake of giving her my number. After that, she acted like my best friend. She'd call or just show up at my door with baked goods or to talk. When I found out she'd moved back, I hoped she wouldn't start doing it again."

"You do have a friendly face. Maybe she doesn't have many friends in the city." A better description would be ruggedly handsome, but for this conversation, friendly would suffice.

"That's what I told myself when she first started doing it. But she lived next door to me for eight months before her company transferred her to their office in New Orleans. So she must know other people besides me."

"If she thought you were involved with someone, she'd probably stop bugging you. And lucky for you, your fake girlfriend is sitting right next to you."

When she was interested in a guy, Tory would make the first

move unless she knew he was involved with someone else. Most of the women she knew were the same way.

"I'm sure I'll see her again this week. When I do, I'll find a way to casually slip your name into the conversation. And if you see her, you should mention me," Tory said.

Maybe their charade would help them both.

SEVEN

A STATE-OF-THE-ART GYM AND AN INDOOR POOL WERE JUST TWO of the many amenities Heritage On The Harbor Terrace offered its residents. Both of which had played a role in Tory's decision to purchase a condo in the building. While there was no shortage of gyms in the city, she loved that a workout was only an elevator ride away. Except for this past week, ever since Tory moved in, she'd gone down every other day. But with Ivy's wedding fast approaching, she'd put exercising on the back burner and focused on work. Her goal had been to switch off her office light on Friday night and not turn it on again until she returned from Puerto Rico.

The late nights, with multiple cups of coffee and chocolate to keep her awake, had paid off. She'd completed everything on her must-do list, and later this morning, she and Duncan were taking the ferry to Sanborn Island like he suggested last weekend.

She hadn't seen him since Saturday night. After watching three episodes of *Lost In Space*, he returned to his place. However, they'd exchanged several text messages during the week. Sometimes they were related to their upcoming trip to Puerto Rico, other times they were about nothing specific. She was looking forward to seeing him later today.

Compared to the pool area, the women's locker room was a walk-in freezer, and despite her towel, goose bumps formed on her arms as soon as Tory stepped back inside. Not surprisingly, she still had the room to herself. After all, it was six thirty on Saturday morning. Most people she knew preferred to start their days a little later during the weekend. If she weren't meeting Duncan at eight, she'd still be upstairs enjoying a coffee before coming down to swim.

"Hey, I haven't seen you at all this week. Were you sick?" someone asked as Tory opened her locker.

Tory glanced toward the door. On the few occasions she'd left her home office all week, she'd kept an eye out for Lori Ann but never saw her. "No, I had a lot of work I needed to finish. My boyfriend and I are going away next week, and I didn't want to take anything with me."

"It's been almost a year since my last vacation. I'm going to see my family in December for the holidays, but that's not a vacation. It's more like an ordeal, if you know what I mean. Hopefully, in January I can get away, though. I have no idea where I'll go," Lori Ann said, setting her bag down and opening the locker next to Tory. "Where are you and your boyfriend off to?"

"Puerto Rico. A good friend of mine from college is getting married there, and I'm her maid of honor."

"I've never been, but I've heard it's beautiful." Lori Ann pulled her T-shirt off, revealing a bright blue bathing suit, and tossed it inside a locker. "Maybe I should go there in January. The weather there will be a lot nicer than here. I hate the cold. I grew up in Miami, Florida. It seldom gets colder than sixty degrees there."

"This will be my first time there, but Duncan's been." Hopefully, mentioning Duncan would be enough to pique Lori Ann's interest, because she couldn't think of a way to include his last name in the conversation without it being awkward.

Lori Ann's eyebrows bunched together. “Does your boyfriend live in the building?”

That was easy enough. “Yep, on the fourth floor. You know him. You brought him cookies two weekends ago. They were delicious, by the way. I'd love to get the recipe.”

“Oh, I didn't realize that was you there that night. I have a cousin named Torrance, but everyone calls him Tory.” Lori Ann's frown disappeared almost as quickly as it appeared. “So I always think of Tory as a guys’ name. Duncan's family often visits, so I thought he had a cousin staying with him for the weekend when he mentioned the two of you were about to eat dinner.”

“It's funny how we do that with names. I always considered Jamie a girls’ name until I worked with a man named James, and everyone called him Jamie. Well, when they weren't calling him some less complimentary names behind his back.”

“Yeah, I thought of Jamie as a girls’ name too until I read a book and the hero was a Scottish laird named Jamie. After that, I never thought of it as a girls’ name again.” Lori Ann shrugged half-heartedly. “How long have you and Duncan been together?”

Their story worked with Duncan's friends at the winery, so she'd use it again now. “We've been together since September, but I've known him a long time. We went to high school together, and my cousin Alec is his close friend. You might know him too. Alec used to live in the building. I actually bought his condo.”

“Oh, yeah. I remember Alec. I was wondering why I hadn't seen him around since I moved back to the area,” Lori Ann said. “Where did he move to?”

“Sanborn Island.”

“I've heard of it, but I've never been.”

“Duncan and I are headed there today.”

“I have to admit, I'm a little jealous of you. Before I moved, Duncan and I were close. We saw each other almost every day. I considered not accepting the promotion because it meant leaving

Boston, and I knew he couldn't move." Lori Ann took off her sweatpants and put them in her locker as she spoke. "We stayed in touch while I was in New Orleans. And he never mentioned that he was seeing anyone. Honestly, when I found out my company was relocating me back to Boston, I'd hoped we could pick up where we left off."

Either Duncan lied last weekend, or Lori Ann was now.

What difference does it make? I'm lying too.

"When I saw him Wednesday night, I got the impression he did too."

In his text on Wednesday, he mentioned Matt was there. If Lori Ann had visited, he hadn't told her. Then again, who Duncan spent his time with wasn't any of her business. Just like who she saw during the week wasn't any of his. Even if she'd had ten different men over this week, she wouldn't owe him an explanation.

"Oh well, I guess I'm not very good at reading men. It wouldn't be the first time I thought someone was interested in more than being friends and it turned out I was wrong." Shrugging, Lori Ann slipped a combination lock on the door. "Hey, if I don't see you again before you leave next week, have a nice vacation."

"Thanks. Enjoy your weekend."

DESPITE THE VOICE telling Tory to forget about it, her conversation with Lori Ann remained annoyingly foremost in her thoughts several hours later. She saw no reason for either party to lie to her, but clearly, one of them had. Whether it had been Duncan or Lori Ann was anyone's guess. And it should not bother her. But, damn, it did.

"There's just something about the ocean," Duncan said as they stepped onto the ferry's open deck. "It relaxes me as nothing else can."

"I don't know why, because I love it, but I didn't go to the beach often when I lived in California, even though it wasn't that far away." She turned and leaned back against the railing. Maybe some people watching would distract her from her conversation this morning with Lori Ann. "The last time I went might have been when I was with Keith. He was big into surfing, and sometimes we'd go to the beach for the day. But it's been over a year since we were together."

"I tried surfing for the first time in the spring. For my parents' wedding anniversary, I took the family to Hawaii. I'd love to try it again."

"Our hotel in Puerto Rico offers lessons. Ivy made sure we weren't doing things as a group 24/7, so you can book a lesson or two while we're there."

Duncan moved so his back was against the railing too and then turned his face toward her. "Is that something you'd be interested in doing?"

"No, I've tried it a few times when I was with Keith and didn't care for it. But that doesn't mean you can't." Even if they were an actual couple, they wouldn't necessarily do everything together while on vacation. "Trust me, I can find something to do for a few hours."

The hotel had a private beach. Tory could picture herself relaxing on a chair while reading a book and working on her tan. Unless she went to a tanning salon, she wouldn't be doing that anytime soon with winter in Boston approaching. Shopping was always an option as well. She loved a good shopping spree. One of the bridesmaids might be interested in joining her.

"I'll think about it. Since it sounds like we'll have some free time, is there anything you want to do while we're there?"

"There are a few historical sites I read about on the internet. Depending on how far away they are from the hotel and how much free time we have, I might visit them."

"When I was there, I didn't get to do much other than attend workshops. But I remember someone mentioning some Spanish fortifications close to the hotel. There is also a small one right next to it. I had a fantastic view of it from my hotel room. One night they even held some kind of concert inside it."

Two children who appeared to be about eleven or twelve years old caught Tory's eye as they walked by them. Or, more specifically, the objects in their hands did. The girl carried what looked like a traditional banana split while her companion had a hot fudge sundae covered with walnuts and chocolate sprinkles.

"Wow, those look amazing. If it wasn't so early, I'd go get a sundae."

"Don't worry, getting ice cream is on the agenda for today. A visit to the island wouldn't be complete without a stop at Sundae Scoops. No one makes better ice cream."

"I'm not sure you're right. Pirate's Cove in Newport has great ice cream. Whenever I'm there, I stop and get some." She'd gone there twice when she'd been in Newport for her cousin's wedding. Once right after checking into her hotel and then again with two of her cousins. "Vanilla Moon in Healdsburg has amazing ice cream too."

"Hey, I've been to Pirate's Cove, and I agree their ice cream is great. Much better than anything you'll buy in a store. And they have a great mini-golf course, but I guarantee Sundae Scoops is better."

The magnetism of his smile had her focusing on his mouth. His oh-so-sensual mouth, and one she'd found herself staring at last weekend too, even though, like now, she shouldn't have been doing it.

Unless she counted the brief contact their lips made on stage as a kiss, which she didn't, she'd never kissed a man with facial hair. And right now, she shouldn't be wondering how it'd feel if they kissed. But, unfortunately, no one had told her silly brain that, and it was wondering with a capital W.

Would his sexy, barely-there beard be rough against her skin, or would it tickle? Would his lips feel as firm as they looked, or would they be soft?

Tory shifted her gaze further north, toward his eyes. "I'm finding that hard to believe. But we'll see."

Before coming on board, they'd bought coffee. Now seemed like as good a time as any to take a sip, since it would give her mouth something to do besides test the firmness of Duncan's lips. The perfect combination of pumpkin, cinnamon, and nutmeg hit her tongue, letting her know she'd made the right decision by going with the pumpkin latte instead of the mocha one.

"Has Lori Ann made any unexpected visits this week?"

She needed to learn to keep her mouth shut.

Duncan nodded as he lowered his coffee cup. "Yeah, on Wednesday night. I was letting Matt in when she walked off the elevator with some pumpkin muffins she'd baked. She hung around for a few minutes and then left. I haven't seen her since then."

His was a slightly different version than the one Lori Ann gave her this morning. So, was Duncan telling her the truth, or was Lori Ann?

It doesn't matter.

They were spending so much time together now to prepare for next week, not because they were dating and wanted to see where things went. In two weeks, Ivy would be married and their agreement would be behind them. So while they might see each other at the gym or maybe meet up for coffee occasionally, they wouldn't be going to wine tastings and dinners. And she certainly wouldn't be staying at his house on Sanborn Island.

"With Matt standing there, I didn't want to mention I was seeing someone. Because then he'd start asking questions, and I don't want to explain it to him too."

She could understand that. Other than Ivy, none of her friends knew the truth, and she intended to keep it that way. "Lori Ann came into the locker room as I was getting ready to leave this morning. I told her we were going to Sanborn today and then on vacation together next week. So, hopefully, she got the message and will leave you alone."

Assuming that's what you want. A man could play hard to get just as easily as a woman. Maybe that was Duncan's game with Lori Ann.

"I guess we'll see."

HOME. The thought washed over him like it always did when he reached the island as the ferry docked, and they joined the line of passengers disembarking.

He lived in Massachusetts, and the state listed him as a resident. However, he considered Sanborn Island home. Even when he'd lived with his parents in Windham, he'd considered Sanborn home.

"How are we getting to your house from here? Are we walking?" Tory asked, walking alongside him. Her arm brushed against his every so often. And each time it did, he wanted to reach down and take her hand like he had last weekend when they had left the winery with Lou and his fiancée.

When possible, Duncan made his life as convenient as possible. So before his last visit, he'd purchased a car to leave on the island, so he didn't need to either bring one over on the ferry when he visited or rent one. Since they still needed to get from the dock to his house, he'd asked his cousin, who was also his neighbor, to pick them up.

"It'd be a long walk, but we could. But since we'd have the suitcases, I asked my cousin Shane to pick us up and bring us to my house. I have a car there we can use to get around. And Shane offered to give us a ride back here tomorrow."

Although not deserted, the crowd waiting to board either a ferry back to the mainland or a charter boat for a day of sightseeing or fishing was nothing like it would've been two months ago. Still, it took Duncan a moment to spot Shane waiting for them.

"Tory is Alec's cousin," he explained after making introductions. When he'd asked Shane to pick them up, he'd only said a friend was coming with him. Duncan hadn't shared that Tory was female or how they knew each other. "Shane and Alec worked together this summer," he added for Tory's benefit.

"You won my cousin at the bachelor auction a couple of weekends ago," Shane commented as they made their way to the parking lot.

Although he'd offered to do it, Tory walked alongside him, pulling her leopard-print suitcase behind her. "I did."

"Please tell me Gianna didn't record the auction and send you a copy."

"If she recorded it, she didn't send me a copy. I checked the foundation's website after the auction to see who you ended up with that night. I hoped to see a photo of you and a grumpy, silver-haired granny. But I wish I'd thought to ask Gianna or Alec to record it so I could see it. I would've even made copies and given them as gifts to everyone for Christmas."

Man, he hoped neither his cousin nor Alec had recorded it. He didn't need a recording of the night being passed around to his sister and all his cousins. "Sorry to disappoint you."

"Maybe Alec recorded it anyway. I'll have to ask him."

Duncan wouldn't put it past his friend. Maybe he should reach out before Shane did, and if Alec had a copy, ask him what he wanted in exchange for destroying it.

"Why in the world did you bid on Duncan, Tory? I saw who else took part that night, and there were some much better options than my cousin. Isn't every woman on Earth in love with Junior Morris? At least that's what my girlfriend tells me."

"Your cousin had the best romantic dates planned out of anyone else there. This weekend trip here is actually one of them. We went on our first date last weekend. Duncan took me to Primrose Winery and then to dinner at Emilia. It's an Italian restaurant in Boston."

She was good at thinking on her feet.

"Duncan Ferguson." Shane clapped him on the shoulder. "This guy right here planned the best romantic dates? Are you sure we're talking about the same person?"

When they reached Shane's SUV, Duncan opened the trunk and put his suitcase in. "Hey, if you ever need help planning something for Monica, you've got my number."

"I don't need help, but if I did, you'd be the last person I called."

"You must get this a lot, but you look just like the actor CJ Ferguson," Tory said, handing Duncan her suitcase. "Seriously, the two of you could be twins."

"He's my older brother," Shane said.

"That explains why you look so much alike." Tory turned her gaze toward him. "I didn't know you were related to him, Duncan."

"Yeah, CJ and Shane's dad, Gianna's, and mine are brothers." Duncan opened the front passenger-side door for her and waited for her to get inside. "My dad is the only one who doesn't still live here."

"I occasionally saw CJ at Anderson Brady's house when we were together."

Much like when she mentioned dating a surfer guy named Keith, his gut twisted into a knot now. "CJ and Anderson have been friends a long time."

"Did CJ get married, or am I confusing him with someone else?" Tory asked.

"Yeah, he got married last year. Neither wanted a media circus, so they had a small wedding ceremony here at his house. Then, about a month later, they had a big formal reception at the Harbor House in Boston."

Duncan had gone to the ceremony at CJ's house but had skipped the big gathering. When he needed to attend large events and interact with people he didn't either know or like, he did. However, he preferred to avoid them. His cousin knew that and had told him he understood if Duncan chose not to come.

"I must have read it somewhere, but I don't remember who he married. Is she an actress?"

A-list actors like his cousin often married other celebrities, so Tory's question was a logical one.

Shane closed the car door and started the engine. "No, Isabelle is a high school history teacher. CJ and Isabelle have known each other forever, and Isabelle's brother is CJ's best friend. They grew up across the street from each other. Her parents and mine are good friends. They even go on vacations together."

"Do CJ and his wife live here?"

"No, CJ and Isabelle live in North Salem. But they have a house here. CJ bought it from Anderson," Shane answered. "They were here all summer and will be back for Thanksgiving. I think they also intend to stay here over the school holiday break in December."

"North Salem. That name sounds familiar for some reason," Tory said.

"Maybe you drove by it. It's about forty minutes from Boston." Pulling out his beeping cell phone, Duncan found a text message from Alec.

I heard you're coming to the island this weekend.

He should've known Shane would tell Gianna he was coming, and of course, she'd tell Alec.

Just got here.

Do you want to come by or meet Gi and me for dinner somewhere?

Tory is with me. I'll check with her.

Since Tory had given him the okay to tell her, Gianna knew what was going on between them, which meant Alec did too.

Let me know.

Returning the device to his pocket, he listened as Shane and Tory discussed their favorite places in Boston.

Duncan could've afforded a multimillion-dollar home like the ones his cousin and Alec owned. When he'd decided to buy a place here, he'd even looked at a few. But not only was he single, but much of his family lived on the island, making a five-thousand-square-foot vacation home with eight bedrooms and nine bathrooms unnecessary. So instead, he'd purchased the sixty-year-old, two-bedroom cottage next to Shane. While it wasn't on the water, he could see the ocean from his backyard. And when he wanted to do more than look at the water, he could walk to the small, secluded beach at the end of the street. Although not private, it didn't appear on any map designed for tourists. Even better, since it didn't have a designated parking area, usually only people who lived in the immediate vicinity used it.

While it was sufficient for his needs, he wondered what Tory would think of it. He'd never seen where she'd lived before moving, but he'd bet his entire stock portfolio it was bigger than the nine-hundred-square-foot cottage with its outdated kitchen he owned here.

Shane stopped in front of the cottage's detached two-car garage, an add-on the previous family had built after they purchased the property from the original owners. "I left some firewood near your back door, but if you need more, just come by and grab some."

The previous owners had used the place mostly only in the summer, so when the furnace had died two years ago, they never replaced it. Instead, they'd relied on the woodstove and electric space heaters if they came in the fall or early spring. He intended to have an HVAC company come in and replace the heating system and install central air, but he hadn't been around enough to get estimates. So if it got chilly tonight, they'd use the woodstove. Even if they didn't need the wood for that, Duncan wanted it for the firepit in the backyard. Since Shane always had firewood on hand, he'd asked if he could have some rather than waste time getting it.

"Tory, if you want more interesting company tonight, my girlfriend and I live next door. We'll be home all night. Just knock on the door."

Tory glanced back at Duncan before smiling at his cousin. "I'll remember that."

EIGHT

THEY'D STAYED AT HIS HOUSE LONG ENOUGH FOR THEM TO PUT their suitcases away and use the bathroom before heading out again. Then, after a tour around the island, Duncan headed to what most people considered downtown. Within walking distance from where the ferries docked, the area contained everything from hotels and restaurants to art galleries. Unless a resident needed something they could only find there, most avoided the area, especially in the summer months. But no first-time visit to the island would be complete without checking out the shops, since many could only be found on the island.

"Do all these shops stay open all year?" Tory asked as they passed Island Wear, a boutique that sold women's clothing, accessories, and shoes.

He never paid attention to which ones stayed open during the off-season. "I think so," he answered, following Tory's lead and stopping in front of a store window.

"That ring is gorgeous." Tory pointed at an aquamarine and diamond ring on display, along with a matching necklace and earrings. "Do you mind if we go inside?"

Duncan had zero interest in jewelry, but he couldn't deny the pieces in the window were beautiful. Even without looking, he knew the items in the shop's other window would be nice too. The mother-daughter team created beautiful pieces. "We can go wherever you want."

He shopped when he needed something and didn't need anything today. But this trip was about Tory, and he wanted her to enjoy herself.

"There's another jewelry store on Front Street; we can check it out too, if you want." He'd noticed Tory always wore different pieces of jewelry. Today she'd gone with an emerald ring and a matching emerald pendant necklace. Last Saturday, she paired her outfit with a simple gold heart pendant, a diamond tennis bracelet, and gold hoop earrings.

"We'll see. I don't need any new jewelry, although I rarely need an excuse to buy more, anyway. Is there anywhere you want to go? I don't want to just go into the stores I want."

Duncan spotted possibly the last person on the island he wanted to see walking toward them. And since his aunt was waving, Duncan knew she'd seen him too. Making an escape into the jewelry store impossible.

"Damn it," he muttered under his breath rather than answer Tory's question as he let go of the store's door handle.

"What's wrong?" Tory asked understandably, sounding confused.

Before he answered her, Aunt Audrey reached them.

"Does Gianna know you're here?" his aunt asked as she hugged him.

"Yes, she knows." Returning the embrace, he kissed his aunt's cheek and then gestured toward Tory. "Aunt Audrey, this is my friend Tory."

He'd lie to Tory's ex and her friends next week about them being together, but he would not lie to his aunt.

"She'd never been to the island, and neither of us had anything else to do this weekend, so we took the ferry over this morning," he continued.

"Welcome. What do you think of Sanborn so far?" Aunt Audrey asked.

"It reminds me a bit of Martha's Vineyard. I see why Duncan likes it here so much."

"I've lived here for over thirty years, so I'm biased, but I've always preferred Sanborn to Martha's Vineyard."

Duncan had yet to meet a resident of Sanborn Island who didn't feel the same way. Himself included. And if you asked someone who called Martha's Vineyard home, they'd probably say they preferred it to Sanborn Island.

"How long are the two of you staying?" His aunt transferred the shopping bags she carried to her other wrist.

"Just the night. We're planning to take the first ferry back in the morning. Tory leaves for vacation on Monday and has some stuff to do at home."

He wasn't lying. Tory was leaving on Monday morning. He'd just failed to add he was traveling with her. And no one, including his Aunt Audrey and his parents, needed to know where he planned to be next week.

"Oh, where are you headed, Tory?"

If you looked up the words "outgoing" and "conversationalist" in a dictionary, you'd see a picture of Aunt Audrey next to both. It didn't matter if she'd just met you five seconds ago or known you for twenty years; she'd stand around and talk your ear off, unlike her husband, who preferred short, to-the-point conversations. Well, unless he was talking about plants. Then the guy could go on forever.

"Puerto Rico. A good friend of mine from college is getting married there next weekend."

"Corey and I went there two years ago. We had a wonderful time. We went to a little hole-in-the-wall café every morning called La Bahía. It wasn't far from our hotel. They had a sponge cake different from anything I'd ever had and the best coffee. If it is still open, I recommend stopping there."

"I'll keep an eye out for it. What hotel did you stay at?"

Even on an island, finding one café would be much easier if you had a general idea of where to look.

"The Condado Hotel and Suites. I don't remember what street it was on, but it was near the water. Corey and I had a great ocean view from our balcony," Aunt Audrey said, looking at her watch. "Yikes, it's later than I thought. I'd love to stay and chat, but I have a few more things to pick up before I head home. Your Uncle Cameron and Aunt Hannah are coming by for dinner. You're welcome to join us. They should be there around six o'clock."

He enjoyed spending time with his family, but if he showed up for dinner with Tory, it would give everyone the wrong idea. Already he doubted his aunt believed Tory and he were only friends—not that he blamed her. Tory was a beautiful woman, and he'd rarely brought anyone to the island. Add to that the fact he'd been single for a long time, and his aunt would most likely believe they were romantically involved. And that meant he'd be getting a call from Mom before the weekend ended, because as soon as Aunt Audrey had a chance, she would be on the phone with her.

He should've thought it through before inviting Tory to spend the weekend on the island. Sanborn was only so big, and it was easy to run into people.

"Thanks for including us, but Alec invited us over tonight." He hadn't accepted or even thought about his friend's invitation since receiving it earlier, but his aunt didn't know that. And even though he'd implied Alec expected them, he hadn't said that, so he wasn't lying to his aunt. And maybe they would decide to go.

"Well, then, I'll see you at Thanksgiving. You are coming, right?"

The location of Thanksgiving dinner rotated each year. Last year, his parents hosted the gathering. This year, it was Aunt Audrey and Uncle Corey's turn. While the turkey she cooked wasn't as tasty as his mom's or Aunt Hannah's, her sweet potato casserole was out of this world and made up for eating semi-dry turkey.

Unless something unforeseen arose, he'd planned to spend several days on the island at Thanksgiving. "I'll be there."

"Great. Say hello to Alec and Gianna for me." Even though she'd already hugged him, Aunt Audrey did it again. The woman was a hugger. "Tory, it was nice meeting you. Have a wonderful vacation. And, hopefully, this won't be your last visit to Sanborn."

Duncan watched his aunt walk away as he opened the door for Tory. When Bellini Jewelry originally opened, it had been half the size it was now and located on Spring Street. Then ten years ago, Scarlet Novak mentioned the store when Marcy Blake asked about a necklace she wore during an interview. Soon after the interview appeared in *Today Magazine* and on its website, business exploded for Bellini Jewelry. The owner, who, along with her daughter, designed all the pieces, moved the store to its current, much larger location on Main Street.

"Was that Gianna's mom?" Tory asked.

"Yep." Duncan followed Tory into the store.

"Their hair and eye color are different, but otherwise, Gianna looks a lot like her mom."

"Everybody says that. Gianna has the same eye color as Uncle Corey, my dad, and our grandmother."

"Explains why yours are almost identical."

Surprised she'd noticed, he nodded as Hazel, the owner's daughter, walked toward them. She wore a white-and-black dress that reminded him of a chessboard, except in this case, the squares varied in size, and it hurt his eyes to look at her, so instead, he focused on her neon pink headband.

"Good afternoon. Are you looking for anything specific today?" Hazel asked, putting a temporary halt to their conversation.

"I'd like to see the aquamarine set in the window."

"Certainly. That's one of our newest pieces."

Although he didn't plan to buy anything, he checked out the jewelry in the display case closest to him while Tory and Hazel spoke. The various gemstones twinkled under the ceiling lights, but one particular ring caught his attention. The stone was like none he'd ever seen. A combination of golden brown and mossy green, the gemstone reminded him of Tory's eyes. Eyes he'd spent far too much time thinking about over the last few days.

Today her eyes appeared more forest green than brown. But the day they went to the winery, the color reminded him of the chestnuts his grandparents always had on hand during the holidays. The ones he only ever saw his grandfather eat.

Tory's eyes weren't the only thing Duncan thought about more than he should, including their relationship. He'd agreed to help Tory because helping people was something he liked to do, not because he hoped it would lead to more than friendship. But, unfortunately, the more time he spent with her, the more his thoughts moved away from friendship and to something more.

When they were together, awkward silences never occurred, and no topics were ever off limits. They'd even discussed politics, a subject he avoided like the plague with most people. Although he hadn't expected it, they had a lot in common, including covering their french fries in salt and vinegar rather than ketchup. However, they disagreed on what to do if salt and vinegar weren't available. Tory insisted using ranch dressing was an acceptable alternative. Duncan preferred to go with mustard. But hey, no one was perfect.

More importantly, he enjoyed her company in a way he hadn't enjoyed being with anyone in longer than he wanted to admit. Even the night they watched old black-and-white television shows after dinner, he'd enjoyed himself and had been in no rush to get home. He liked how she teased him and listened when he spoke rather than just nodding in agreement, something he'd found more than one date doing. He wasn't proud of it, but he'd done the same thing a few times when his dates started talking nonstop about themselves or fashion. He didn't understand how anyone could care so much about fashion.

If Tory had never asked for his help, he'd consider steering them toward something more than friendship and see what happened. But she had asked.

Just because Tory had ended her last relationship didn't mean she was looking to get involved with someone else. Some people preferred to be single and just go on casual dates rather than sit at home alone every Saturday night. And if Tory were in the market for a relationship, she'd shown no signs that she wanted more from him than friendship. Hell, she might not even want that from him. Everything that had transpired between them so far might be like a dress rehearsal for the following week.

He'd been burned in relationships by women who either wanted or needed something from him. Already he knew Tory wanted something from him. After he fulfilled his end of the bargain, an elevator ride down to the lobby might be the most time they ever spent together again.

In the long run, it might be a mistake, but for now, he'd leave the ball in her corner.

"WHOEVER OWNS Furever Friends should look into opening one in Boston. It would do fantastic, I think. There are so many pet owners in the city. I can see a lot of them wanting to stop and have a snack with their dog while out for a walk. Or picking up a special treat for them on their way home from work. If I owned a dog, I would."

Owned by two sisters, Furever Friends Café and Bakery wasn't the only café on the island. But since it opened five years ago, it had become one of the most popular ones, especially for those who had four-legged friends at home. The establishment was not only pet friendly, but it sold a wide variety of baked goods and drinks prepared for customers with tails and paws and those without any. And when you went inside, you almost always found both human and canine customers enjoying something. This afternoon, it'd been one of their last stops before returning to his house.

"I'm surprised someone hasn't already opened something similar," Tory said.

Confident the fire wouldn't go out, Duncan stood and brushed his hands off on his jeans. "I agree with you. But owning a business in Boston is an entirely different beast from running one here. I'm not sure Melody and Stacey would want to deal with it."

The previous owners had done little to the cottage itself while they owned it. However, they had installed a fabulous patio with a firepit built into the center and a covered grill area just off the house. The weather tonight cried out for an outside fire. And since the old owners had included the five-piece outdoor sofa set in the sale, they had a place to sit while enjoying it.

"Boston is a unique place, that's for sure. New York City isn't perfect, but it's at least easy to find your way around. Boston, forget it. It's like whoever laid out the roads wanted people to get lost."

He'd noticed the same thing when he first moved to Boston for college. Now, he didn't think much about it anymore.

"And no one looks before they cross the street. They just step off the sidewalk and expect the cars to stop. If you honk the horn, people either walk slower to annoy you or flip you the bird," Tory continued.

Duncan considered his many seating options. He could sit across from her with the fire pit between them. Or he could opt for a closer spot and see what happened.

His body decided before his conscience did, and he lowered himself down next to her.

"Do you wish you'd stayed in California?" Life was all about choices. Sometimes you regretted the ones you made, and other times you celebrated them. He'd done his fair share of both over the years.

Tory didn't hesitate to answer. "No. Moving to Boston was the best decision I've made in a long time. And I didn't mean to make it sound as if I hate Boston. There are a lot of things I love about it, including the food in the North End. And there is so much history there. But driving isn't one of them."

"I agree with you on the food and the driving." Why she considered it the best decision she'd made wasn't any of his business. The sound of a car pulling into his driveway stopped him from opening his big trap and asking her regardless. "Sounds like the pizzas are here. I'll be right back."

NOT FOR THE FIRST TIME, she studied his retreating form. Or, more specifically, his ass. The man clearly did a lot of squats and deadlifts.

Before she could stop it, an image of him naked formed. While it might not be 100 percent accurate, she had perfect eyesight, and Duncan did more than sit behind a desk all day and stare at a computer screen.

Bad idea. Yep, she shouldn't imagine Duncan naked. But she was.

"Feel free to start without me. I'll be right back." Duncan set down the takeout order and headed into the house.

This time, she successfully kept her eyes on the fire rather than follow him. By the time he returned with wine and two glasses, she'd removed the tantalizing image of Duncan minus his clothes from her head. Unfortunately, she suspected it would return sooner than later.

"What's your final verdict on the island?" Duncan asked as he handed her a glass. "And if you say you like Martha's Vineyard better, you'll have to find yourself another date for the wedding," he added before she could swallow her mouthful of pizza and answer.

"I definitely don't like Martha's Vineyard better." Tory fought the smile wanting to break free. "But Block Island is another story."

Duncan lowered his glass away from his mouth. "You like Block Island better? That's like a person saying they prefer a Ford Pinto to a Chevy Corvette."

She had no idea what a Ford Pinto looked like, but the name had her envisioning one ugly car.

"If you're serious, I don't think I can even be your friend, never mind your fake boyfriend."

Duncan would never be as close a friend as Leah, but Tory valued the friendship developing between them. And even though she knew he was teasing, a wave of sadness washed over her at the thought of them no longer being friends.

"Relax. I'm kidding." Tory's hand covered his before she realized her intention. "I've never even been to Block Island. But I see why you love it here so much, and sometime this summer, I want to come back and see more of the island."

"Our friendship is safe for now." Duncan raised his glass again and took a sip.

Somewhat mesmerized, Tory watched the flames dance and smoke rise into the night sky for the next few minutes as they ate in silence.

"I've never sat outside by a fire like this." She placed her empty paper plate on the table rather than get another slice of pizza. They'd bought ice cream on the way back, and it was waiting for them in the freezer.

"Never?" The way Duncan said the word, one might think she'd told him she'd never experienced a thunderstorm.

"A firepit like this wouldn't exactly fit in the yards at any of my parents' estates." Even if it did, neither of her parents would ever use it. She doubted either even knew how to start a fire.

"You never went camping when you were younger?"

"My family isn't the camping type. Mom considers a hotel without a full-service spa roughing it." She liked her creature comforts too. However, what Tory considered a necessity and what Mom did were vastly different. "Dad isn't much better."

Tory glanced at him in time to catch Duncan's smile. "We camped all the time. Mom and Dad still go camping a few times a year. You don't know what you're missing."

She understood the appeal of sitting by a fire like this but saw nothing enjoyable about sleeping on the ground in a tent. "I'll take your word for it. I don't need a hotel with a spa, but I don't want to sleep on the ground either and get wet if it rains or attacked by mosquitoes."

"Sometimes I'd sleep outside in a tent to get away from my sister, but we had a camper. It even had a television, although Mom and Dad never let my sister and I use it. Not even when it rained; instead, we'd play board games or cards."

That sounded much better than in a tent on the ground. "That kind of camping I think I could handle."

Especially if you were with me.

She shouldn't be entertaining thoughts like that. But what you shouldn't do and what you did weren't always the same.

"There are plenty of campgrounds in New England. Several have campers on-site that you can use. Some have small rustic cabins you can stay in too. Usually, they have electricity but not a bathroom. At a few campgrounds, they even have small, hotel-room-sized refrigerators. So if you ever want to try camping, I can give you a list of places." Standing, Duncan stacked the pizza boxes. "Do you want more wine, or are you ready to try the best ice cream in the world?"

"Ice cream."

Tory almost got up and followed him inside the house. But instead, she watched the fire and reminded herself she needed his help. If she kissed him tonight, he might back out of their agreement.

Or he might kiss me back.

Usually, she could read men. But not Duncan. Sometimes he treated her like a buddy—someone you went to a baseball game with or met for lunch. A few times, though, she'd seen the heat in his eyes when he looked at her.

"You look like you're contemplating the meaning of life."

I was just contemplating you. "Just zoned out. The fire is kind of hypnotic."

"It can be." Sitting down, he handed her an enormous bowl of ice cream covered with whipped cream. "Tell me what you think." He nodded toward her bowl before digging into his even larger serving.

Rich, dark chocolate and coconut teased her taste buds, and Tory closed her eyes. "You weren't kidding."

Duncan's laugh sent shivers down her spine. "If you haven't noticed yet, I'm usually right."

Tory prepared herself for his smile before opening her eyes. Only it wasn't his smile that captured her attention. Instead, it was his eyes and the desire reflected in them.

Heat hotter than what the fire was giving off swept through her. "Is that so?" She leaned toward him.

"It is."

Whether he moved or she did, the gap between them became smaller.

Pop!

Startled, Tory jumped back, breaking whatever spell they'd been under. "What the heck was that?"

"Don't worry. Nothing is wrong. It happens when steam is released from the wood." Duncan brought a spoonful of ice cream to his mouth.

Without a doubt, Duncan's mouth would be against hers instead of his spoon if not for the fire. Either the wood had the best timing in the world or the worst. Right now, she wasn't sure which it was.

NINE

A CRYSTAL-CLEAR, BLUE SKY AND A TROPICAL BREEZE GREETED Tory and Duncan when they exited the hotel's parking garage. Considering that they would spend much of their time at the resort, and they could use a car service if they wanted to leave, a rental car wasn't necessary. Regardless, she'd gotten them one for the week. She enjoyed having the ability to come and go without depending on anyone else.

"I think the weather here is slightly better than at home." Tory stopped at the curb and waited for an opportunity to cross the street.

It had been thirty-two degrees and pouring when they entered Logan Airport this morning. The cold she could tolerate, especially if she dressed accordingly. The rain she didn't mind, especially if she didn't have to drive in it. But she hated it when the two combined.

"Can't argue with you there," Duncan replied as they crossed the street and walked onto the hotel's property.

A sprawling complex, the hotel consisted of five buildings with an open lobby placed in the middle of them. Various restaurants and stores occupied the ground-floor level in two of the buildings, while a full-service spa and ballrooms were in two of the other ones. Tory had yet to learn what the deal was with the fifth building. Near the tennis courts, the structure consisted of only two floors and was a short walk away from the others.

Tory kept an eye out for Grant or anyone else from the wedding party as they crossed the lobby and joined the guests waiting to speak with someone at the front desk. She could handle being surprised by one of the bridesmaids. But she wanted to be prepared to see Grant.

She spotted Ivy and Preston walking out of the sandwich shop and waved as she took back her driver's license and a credit card from the hotel employee.

"I see you are staying with us until the twenty-third," the hotel employee said. "How many room keys would you like?"

They'd be spending a lot of time together, but they wouldn't be attached at the hip. "Two, please."

After jotting down the suite number, the employee put the key holder and a resort map on the desk. "Your suite is in the Wave Rider Tower," the employee said, circling one of the many buildings featured on the map. "The hotel offers a variety of free activities every day. You will find them posted on the display screens around the resort. You can also find them on Channel 5. No reservations are required for them. The hotel's fitness center is open twenty-four hours a day, and it is here." The woman circled the two-story building near the tennis courts. "Our tennis courts are free to use; however, you'll need to reserve a court in advance."

Even if Tory had known the hotel had tennis courts, she wouldn't have brought her racket. At home, she could easily find a place to play tennis. But, unfortunately, she couldn't tour an almost five-hundred-year-old Spanish fortification just anywhere. And El Morro in Old San Juan was on her list of places to visit while here.

Almost as soon as they stepped away from the front desk, Ivy threw her arms around Tory. "You're here! How was your flight?"

"Uneventful." Just the way she liked her flights to be.

Before she could make introductions, Ivy smiled and hugged Duncan. The woman didn't have a shy bone in her body and treated everyone as if they were her best friend. "It's nice to finally meet you, Duncan. Tory has told me a lot about you."

She hadn't spoken to Ivy about Duncan except to tell her he was coming. So Tory assumed Ivy had made the comment for Preston's sake, because if they were a couple, Tory would've shared many of the details of their relationship with her friend.

Duncan didn't let it show if Ivy's hug made him uncomfortable. Instead, he smiled and returned the embrace. "Tory talks about you all the time. I feel like I already know you."

Another untrue statement, but like Ivy, he'd said it for Preston's sake.

"Duncan, this is my fiancé, Preston." Ivy slipped her arm around Preston's waist.

If Preston was anything, it was welcoming, and he extended his hand toward Duncan. "It's nice to meet you. I'm glad you could join us."

"Where is your room?" Ivy asked once introductions were out of the way.

"We're in the Wave Rider Tower." Tory opened the cardholder to check their room number. "Suite 1403."

"Awesome. We're neighbors. Preston and I are in 1405. Hayden and Gab are in our tower too, but they're on the seventh floor."

Since Hayden had also gone to college with Tory and Ivy, she'd known her the longest of all the women in the bridal party. Until a year ago, the woman had been married to her college sweetheart. Unfortunately, her frequent travel for work and her husband's inability to be faithful when she wasn't around ended their twelve-year relationship last year.

Although she rarely got involved in her friends' relationships, Tory had introduced Hayden and Gab to each other. A coworker at Desjardin, Gab was a great guy with a heart of gold.

But, unfortunately, he always seemed to attract women who abused his generosity.

When Hayden had announced she was ready to date about six months ago, Tory set up a blind date between her two friends. They'd been together ever since.

"Who else has arrived?"

Ivy had asked everyone to arrive today, but since the first scheduled event wasn't until this evening, there was still plenty of time for people to show up.

"Madeline and Ted got here yesterday. I haven't seen Carrie and Drake, but she texted me about an hour ago that they had checked in. Olivia's flight doesn't get in until four."

Well, that took care of the bridal party and one groomsman. But what about the rest?

"Steve and his girlfriend are down at the pool. We're heading back there; we offered to grab lunch for everyone. None of us felt like anything on the menu out there. Andrew and his wife should be landing about now."

That explained the multiple bags Preston carried.

"Grant texted Preston about ten minutes ago to let us know he checked in. He might come down to the pool after he unpacks," Ivy continued. "Beau and his fiancée got here about half an hour ago. They're going to meet us at the pool for lunch. If they're not already there, they should be soon." Wedding bells erupted from Ivy's cell phone, and she removed it from her coverup. "Preston, Steve wants to know if we want anything from the bar."

"Tell him to get me whatever he's having."

"I made a list of where everyone's room is. I just sent it to you." After replying to Steve and sending Tory the list via text message, Ivy returned the phone to her pocket. "After you unpack, join us at the pool. We'll be there for a while."

If Grant might join everyone out there, Tory would find something else to do. Sure, she'd have to deal with him eventually, but she'd put it off for as long as possible. "Maybe."

"Well, if you don't come down, we'll see you at six o'clock. You got the itinerary I sent this morning, right?"

"I got the one you sent last week." She'd glanced over it and then saved a copy on her phone. Not that she needed to do that. Knowing Ivy, she would hand out copies to everyone tonight at dinner.

"I sent you an updated one this morning when we arrived."

She hadn't checked her email yet today. "When I get upstairs, I'll download the new one. Is dinner still at the same time and same place?"

"Yep."

"Great. If we don't see you at the pool, we'll see you at dinner."

Parting ways, Ivy and Preston headed in one direction while Tory and Duncan went in another.

Stepping inside the elevator, Duncan pressed the button for the fourteenth floor as a woman accompanied by two teenagers entered right after them. "What floor?" he asked.

"Looks like you already got it. We're headed to the fourteenth floor too. Are the two of you just checking in?"

Since they had suitcases with them, it seemed like a silly question, but Tory saw no reason to be rude. "Yes. How long have you been here?"

"We got here on Friday afternoon. We come here every year on a family vacation, although we usually come in January." She gestured toward the teens as she continued. "The boys made the ski team this year, so a January vacation is out."

If the woman and her family came that often, they'd probably visited much of the island. Even if they hadn't, they might have some favorite places to visit. "Are there any places you think we should visit while we're here?"

"I recommend the rain forest. The Arenales Caves are great too. And if you like seafood, you need to go to La Parrilla."

"Last year, we went on trails using ATVs. It was a lot of fun," the taller of the two teens said.

"That's right. We did. We used a company called Tropical Adventures. You can book everything through their website."

Ivy had penciled in some free time. There wouldn't be enough to fit all that, but it gave her a place to start. "Thank you for the suggestions."

The elevator doors opened to a colorful lobby with hallways extending in two directions. According to the sign, suites 1401 through 1409 were down on the left.

"Our suite is this way," Tory said.

Photos depicting various spots in and around the hotel, as well as El Yunque National Rain Forest, decorated the hallway walls.

Duncan gestured toward one photo hung near the door when they reached their suite. "That's the fort I told you I could see from my hotel room the last time I was here."

Before opening the door, she glanced at the photo. "It's called San Gerónimo. After you told me about it, I looked it up. Depending on when it's open, I'm planning to visit it." Since it was so close, a quick visit should be easy, and its size meant it wouldn't take all day to explore.

Colorful furniture filled the living room area when they walked inside, and a small kitchen, a half bathroom, and stairs to the second level were located off to their right. Additional chairs and a small table were on the balcony, and Tory pictured herself sitting out there in the morning while enjoying her coffee. Or maybe even later tonight, when they returned from dinner with some tea.

"I'm more than happy to go with you if you want company." Duncan followed her up the stairs to the second level and stopped on the landing. "Which room do you want?"

Both rooms had their own bathroom and access to the second-level balcony. The only difference between them was that one had a king-size bed while the other contained two queen-sized ones. Of course, since she'd be sleeping alone, the bed size made little difference to her.

"Doesn't matter to me."

"You pick," Duncan replied.

"I'll take this one." She gestured toward the door on her right, since it was closer to her. "It shouldn't take me long to unpack." Some people lived out of their suitcases while on vacation. Not her. She liked everything in its place. Tory even needed her toiletries and makeup put away before she did anything else while away from home.

"Yeah, it won't take me long either. I know you don't want to meet your friends at the pool when we're done, but is there anything you want to do before dinner?"

"Wait a minute. I never said I didn't want to join everyone at the pool."

"That's true. You said maybe, but I knew what you were thinking."

She hated when people made comments like that, even though in this case, Duncan was right. When she'd told Ivy maybe, she'd had no intentions of meeting everyone after they unpacked.

But how had he known what she was thinking? Had he developed mind-reading abilities? If so, Tory was in big trouble, because she didn't need Duncan knowing how much she thought about him. Especially since some of those thoughts had him wearing far less clothing than he was now.

"I'll think about it while I put my things away."

DUNCAN OPENED the sliding glass door and stepped outside rather than grab something to eat from the kitchen, which his stomach was urging him to do. When Tory told him she'd arranged to have food delivered to their suite, she hadn't been kidding. The fridge contained fresh fruits, milk, juice, and water. A loaf of bread, a package of bagels, and bananas were on the counter. Two kinds of cereal, peanut butter, and various snacks were in the two cupboards. He hadn't looked, but it wouldn't surprise him if more food were in the freezer. And if they weren't heading down to dinner soon, he'd pour himself a bowl of cereal and eat it with some fresh strawberries. But dinner was in less than twenty minutes, and unfortunately, Mom had drilled into him not to ruin his appetite before a meal.

Resting his forearms on the balcony railing, he looked down at the old fort while he enjoyed the tropical breeze. Earlier, when they finished unpacking, they'd walked over to San Gerónimo. Unfortunately, they'd arrived ten minutes late, and it'd already closed for the day. So rather than return to their suite, they'd visited the hotel's tropical garden and bird sanctuary before stopping at Caribe Water Adventures to see what they offered. He had booked nothing because, honestly, he'd been unable to decide between the scuba lessons and the sea trekking. Tory had made no reservations either but told him she was interested in the sea trekking or the snorkeling. Afterward, they'd gone to the hotel's patio café for coffee, but neither had ordered food, even though the display case had some delicious-looking baked goods—something he was kicking himself for now.

"I wouldn't mind having this view every day."

At the sound of Tory's voice, Duncan turned his head. "Yeah, I know what you mean," he agreed, although right now they were referring to very different views.

Whenever he saw Tory, she looked great. Tonight wasn't any different. Her white sundress was held up by thin spaghetti straps and ended two or three inches above the knee. She'd taken down her hair since he'd last seen her, and it hung loose, cascading over her shoulders. And now, like the last time she'd worn her hair down while with him, he wanted to run his fingers through it and see if it was as soft as it looked.

"Sorry it took me so long to get ready." Tory stopped next to him and put her hands on the railing. "I had trouble deciding what to wear."

Duncan wouldn't be the only one at the restaurant who couldn't take his eyes off her tonight. "You look fantastic."

"Thanks. You clean up pretty well yourself." Smiling, she nudged his arm with her elbow. "Before I came down, I emailed you Ivy's updated itinerary for the week. I haven't looked at it yet, because I know she'll review it tonight. If we still have some free time in the morning, do you want to walk over to the fort again with me after breakfast?"

The sign on the gate had stated it would be open tomorrow and Thursday from nine until two. Then, on Wednesday and Friday, it was open from twelve to five.

"Sounds good to me. Then, if we have time on Wednesday, we can drive over to El Morro."

"I'll have to double-check Ivy's schedule. I think the guys are going golfing on Wednesday, and the women are having a spa day, or maybe that was Friday. I know golfing was on there somewhere."

"We're not doing everything as a group?"

"Nope. Sorry, I thought I mentioned that. But don't worry, you'll get along fine with everyone except possibly Grant."

Gee, I wonder why? "I'll survive."

"If you're ready, we should go."

"I'm all set, but you don't sound it."

Sighing, Tory tilted her head back, exposing her neck, and he envisioned himself leaving a trail of kisses from her collarbone and to her lips. Once he learned the taste of her, he'd reverse his path.

"After traveling, I like to relax. And if we were here for a vacation, I'd suggest we get room service and eat it out here. And then maybe go for a walk on the beach."

Before he did something he shouldn't, Duncan forced the image away. Even if she was receptive to turning their fake relationship into a real one, something he sometimes sensed she was, now wasn't the time. Her friends expected them for dinner.

"I get it."

The plane ride had only been about four hours. But there was more to traveling than just the plane ride; if you took all of it into account, they'd spent much of their day getting here.

"Room service is out tonight, but we can go for a walk on the beach after dinner if you want."

Lowering her head, Tory looked at him and smiled before stepping away from the railing. "I think I would."

Unlike earlier when they'd shared part of the elevator ride down with newlyweds who couldn't keep their hands off each other, Duncan and Tory thankfully had the elevator to themselves this time. Duncan had no problem with public displays of affection, but those two had taken it to a whole other level.

Tory slipped her hand into his as the elevator doors opened, and in response, his heart skipped a beat. "Showtime," she whispered, her voice just loud enough for him to hear her.

A woman holding hands with a tall blond built like a football player smiled and waved when she stepped out of the elevator next to theirs. "Tory, I thought you'd come and join us at the pool." But unlike when they ran into Ivy, this woman didn't throw her arms around Tory.

"Duncan and I wanted to explore a little. So we went to the garden and then looked into booking either scuba lessons or snorkeling," she said before introducing him to Carrie and her husband, Drake.

"Well, we'll have to catch up later. I feel like I haven't seen you in ages. I can't believe my baby brother is getting married," Carrie said as the two couples walked through the hotel lobby.

"Don't let Preston hear you say that. He hates it when you call him your baby brother," Tory said.

"Why do you think I say it? I'm five minutes older than Preston, Duncan," Carrie explained.

"And she never lets him forget it," Tory added.

"He would do the same to me if he'd been born first."

Duncan didn't know where everything on Ivy's itinerary was taking place, but at least dinner was at the resort. Tory and Carrie were still discussing Preston when they arrived at Baudin's Steak House, a well-known, upscale restaurant with locations in major US cities and large resorts like this one.

"We're part of the Nelson/Turner party," Tory told the restaurant employee once they walked inside the restaurant.

"Most of your party has already been seated. Please follow me."

The employee led them to a private function room where four couples, including the bride and groom, sat enjoying drinks. Before Tory could introduce him to everyone there, three more people joined them, leaving only one person not there yet.

"Is Grant here?" Olivia, the only person at the table without a companion, asked.

"He got here this afternoon," Preston answered. "I don't know why he's not here now."

"Knowing our cousin, he's still doing his hair," Carrie said. "The guy uses more hair gel than I do."

"If he's not here in five minutes, we'll order appetizers without him," Preston said.

Less than a minute after Preston spoke, the same employee escorted Grant into the room. Sure enough, the guy's hair looked like he'd spent time putting each blond strand in its proper place.

So you're Grant. Duncan put his hand over the one Tory had resting on the table.

"Sorry I'm late."

"Admit it. You just wanted to make an entrance," Carrie said, reaching for her water.

"I needed to stop somewhere before I came down." Left with no other option, Grant pulled out the chair next to Olivia as he glanced around the table. His eyes darted back and forth between Duncan and Tory, then to their joined hands as he sat.

"Grant, I think you know everyone here except Gab and Duncan," Preston said.

"Actually, Gab and I've met." Grant glanced at Tory as he

spoke before looking in Duncan's direction again. “I used to see him when I stopped to visit Tory at work.”

The guy wanted Duncan to know he and Tory had a shared past. He could respect that. But it didn't change the fact Tory wanted nothing to do with Grant now. Or that Tory would be spending much of her time with him this week and not Grant.

TEN

IF LOOKS COULD KILL, DUNCAN WOULD'VE BEEN DEAD AND buried even before their appetizers arrived. Based on how Grant had looked at her tonight, he wasn't all that happy with her either. But, as far as Tory was concerned, that was his problem, not hers. She'd made it clear to him it wasn't working out when she ended their relationship. It wasn't her fault if he'd failed to accept that.

"I have copies of this week's itinerary for everyone." Ivy retrieved a leather portfolio from the bag she'd used to carry the gifts for the wedding party and handed a stack of papers to Carrie, who took one and passed the remaining ones on to her neighbor.

"If you didn't look at the new one I emailed this morning, there are a few changes from the original. Instead of going to the rain forest tomorrow, we reserved a beach cabana for the day. That way, we can hang out and relax. But we're still going to the Brazilian grill for dinner."

Good, that would give her and Duncan even more free time to visit the fortification next door after breakfast.

"Wednesday, you have most of the day to yourself. Then

we'll meet in the lobby at seven and head over to the karaoke bar."

You couldn't cancel that too?

"Weren't we going to a zip lining and ropes course on Wednesday?" Steve asked, taking a laminated schedule and then passing the rest to Tory.

"Someone at the table got cold feet about going, so we canceled," Ivy answered.

"And that someone is sitting next to me." Preston pointed toward his fiancée.

"So, sue me. I like a little more than rope under my feet when I'm that high up," Ivy shrugged. "Besides, if anyone wants to go, they have time."

Tory had been looking forward to going, but it was something she could do at home. But if she had all day Wednesday to herself, she could visit El Morro and maybe Castillo San Cristóbal, another old Spanish fortification in San Juan.

"We are still going on the rum distillery tour Thursday, but we'll meet in the lobby at eleven instead of noon."

Tory had only ever been on wine-tasting tours and wondered how a rum tour would compare to them.

"The golf outing, spa day, and rehearsal dinner are still set for Friday."

She'd been wrong about the day, but Duncan would still have to spend the day alone with Grant and the other guys.

"Sounds like it's going to be a great week," Olivia said.

"It's going to be a fun time," Carrie said before covering a yawn and pushing her chair back. "Drake and I have been up since four o'clock, so we'll see everyone tomorrow sometime after breakfast."

"I'm going to head out too. I still need to finish unpacking," Olivia, Ivy's cousin, said, following Carrie's lead and pushing her chair back.

Within a few minutes, only Tory, Duncan, and Grant remained at the table with the future Mr. and Mrs. Turner.

"Do you still want to go for a walk on the beach, Tory?"

She nodded as she gathered up her nifty laminated itinerary —only Ivy would print out the schedule on stationary decorated with pink roses and laminate it—and her present. "I want to bring these up to our room first."

Grant once again shot daggers in Duncan's direction.

Tory waited for Duncan to push his chair in before taking his hand. "Duncan and I are going to visit the fort next door after breakfast. Afterward, we'll join everyone at the beach."

"Take your time. Tomorrow is all about relaxing," Ivy said.

The elevator door opened just as she heard Grant call out to her. Tory briefly considered acting like she hadn't heard him and just getting inside. But she knew Grant. All that would do was postpone the conversation.

"So close," Duncan whispered in her ear as he put an arm over her shoulders and pulled her against his side.

"Tory, I stopped by your room before dinner, but you weren't there. I hoped we could talk."

"How did… never mind," Tory said, remembering Ivy had sent her a list of where everyone's room in the resort was located —a list she hadn't bothered to open. If she'd sent it to Tory, she'd sent it to everyone in the wedding party. "I'm here now, and I'm listening."

Grant's gaze moved to Duncan. "Can we talk alone?"

Other than being annoyed, she saw no harm in talking to him. "Duncan, do you mind bringing this stuff up to our suite while Grant and I talk? And then meet me back here so we can go to the beach."

Grant clenched his jaw as Duncan kissed her temple and accepted the items she held out. "Sure. I'll be right back."

So they weren't in the way of other guests, she walked to the bench opposite the elevators and sat.

"We could've gone up to my room. We'd have more privacy there." Grant sat close to her, and Tory immediately put some space between them.

Shrugging, she glanced around. At the moment, the area was empty except for the woman leaving the middle elevator and walking away. “No one will bother us here.”

The muscle in his cheek twitched, but Grant didn't argue. “I didn't know you were bringing someone this week.”

Well, that wasn't the opening she'd expected. She'd assumed Ivy had mentioned it to Grant. The man was no stranger at their house.

“I hoped we could spend this week working on our relationship.”

“Grant, we've been over this. We're not right for each other, so we have nothing to work on this week or ever.”

“Of course we are. We have many of the same friends. Our families have been close forever. They even have homes near each other.”

“You're right about those things, and maybe that's enough for you, but it isn't enough for me. I want someone who shares some of my interests. Someone who makes me smile and will watch old black-and-white TV shows with me.” Something Grant had always refused to do.

“How can you know if Duncan is ‘right’ for you?” Grant asked, making air quotes. “You've only known the guy for, what, a month? If even that long.”

“I have known Duncan since high school.” How long she'd known someone wasn't any of Grant's business, but she rattled off the story she and Duncan had agreed upon after the auction.

“Fine. You've known him a long time. But that doesn't mean you're right for each other the way we are.” Grant gestured back and forth between them before placing a hand on her shoulder.

Annoyed, she wanted to stomp her foot because the man once again refused to listen. But instead, she removed Grant's hand and counted to ten rather than tell him he was being a stubborn jerk.

“Tory, come on, be reasonable. We belong together. I know it. Both of our families know it, and if you give us another chance, you'll realize it too." Once again, he reached out as if to touch her, but she moved, putting herself just out of his reach.

How many more times do I need to tell you this? "You and our families can believe whatever you want, Grant. But I know we're not right for each other." She pointed toward herself to emphasize her point. "That's all that matters to me."

"But Duncan is?" The muscle in his cheek twitched again as a sliver of anger seeped into his voice.

"Duncan doesn't change the facts about us. But yeah, I think we are right for each other. We like many of the same things, and I enjoy spending time with him." The truth behind the words hit her over the head like a sledgehammer. But she'd have to analyze them later. "I don't know where things will eventually go between Duncan and me, but I know a relationship between you and me will never work."

The elevator doors once again opened, and the topic of their conversation exited, carrying two bottles of water.

"Are you ready to go, or should I come back?" Duncan asked.

"We're not done yet. Tory will find you when we are," Grant replied before she could say anything.

Grant could be full of himself, but until now, she'd never seen him act rude or condescending.

"Nope, we're all set." Standing, Tory kissed Duncan's cheek and put her arm around his waist.

"Tory." Grant's nostrils flared as his lips flattened into a rigid line and he stood.

She didn't care if Grant's head was about to explode. She was done with their conversation. "Is one of those waters for me?"

"Yeah, I thought we might want something to drink while we walk."

"Great minds think alike. I was going to stop in the store and grab a bottle of water before heading out." Tory kissed his cheek again and accepted a bottle. "Have a pleasant evening. We'll see you tomorrow."

"Grant, it was nice meeting you."

"Likewise." If any more sarcasm dripped from Grant's voice, she'd be able to see it. "You and I will have to finish our conversation later, Tory."

Not if I can help it. No matter what Tory said, it wouldn't change his mind tonight. The man was too pigheaded, so she didn't even try.

TORY KEPT her arm around him as they exited the lobby. And it remained there as they walked past one of the hotel's three pools. Since there was no way Grant could still see them, there was no reason for her to keep it there. But if Tory hadn't realized that, Duncan sure as hell would not tell her because, damn, he loved the way she felt pressed against his side.

Earlier, guests both old and young had occupied the area. Now only a few people used the chairs around the pool, although he could see other couples on the walkway along the water and some using the seats situated along it. From here, it was difficult to tell, but he thought there was even someone using a hammock set up in an area of trees close to the beach.

Tory stopped when they reached the spot where the walkway ended and the beach started. "There is nothing like walking in the sand barefoot."

Using his arm for balance, she took off her wedged sandals, or whatever they were called. His sister would know their proper name.

Sand against bare feet was one thing. Sand in your shoes was another. Removing his boat shoes, he walked alongside Tory.

Their conversation wasn't any of his business, but he still wondered what they'd discussed. However, he wouldn't push the matter if Tory told him she didn't want to talk about it.

"What did Grant want?" The guy had looked ready to burst a

blood vessel when Duncan had returned from their suite and joined them.

"Same as always. He insists we belong together and that if I give us another chance, I'll eventually realize it too."

He'd only spent a few hours with Grant, but he didn't like him. But, that aside, he couldn't fault the man for wanting Tory in his life, because it was what Duncan wanted too—and not as a friend, like he'd told his cousin and Alec.

"I've known him forever, and I don't remember him ever being so pigheaded."

Duncan had a more colorful adjective in mind to describe Grant's behavior, but pigheaded would do.

They left the beach and walked onto the circular dock that jutted into the water. Seating ran around the edge, giving guests a place to sunbathe or read a book. They could even have food delivered to them. And if a person got too warm, they could jump in the ocean and cool off. Tory and Duncan had the area to themselves, except for a couple cuddling in one corner.

"At dinner, I got the impression Ken didn't know you were coming with someone."

"Ken? Is there something other than water in that bottle?"

To him, his comment made sense, but he understood why it didn't to Tory. "My sister went through a Barbie phase. Grant reminds me of Ken with his perfect hair. Does the guy own a hair gel company or something?"

Tory burst out laughing. "He's always been particular about his appearance. And now, thanks to you, whenever I see him, I will want to call him Ken." She stopped about halfway around the dock. "Let's sit here."

"Grant didn't know you'd be here with me this week. Did you see his face when he first saw you? I think he might have cracked a few teeth."

"Yeah, he was not a happy camper tonight."

Thanks to the moonlight and stars, he could see her well.

"You should've seen him when he asked if I thought you

were right for me, and I told him yes. I thought his head was going to explode." Leaning toward him, she put her hand on his arm, branding him. "And when I told him I enjoyed spending time with you, I wasn't lying."

During dinner, he'd reached a decision. He'd keep the status quo until they returned to Boston. Then he'd let Tory know where his head was at and see if she was on the same page.

Following through on his plan was beyond him now. Before common sense returned, he closed the gap between them and kissed her, lingering and savoring every moment of his lips against hers.

The hunger pulsing through his body urged him to deepen the kiss, coax her lips apart, and learn the taste of her. Instead, he pulled back and brushed his fingers against her jaw before slipping them through her hair—hair far softer than he'd imagined.

Duncan waited until Tory met his eyes before speaking. "I know what I agreed to. But, Tory, everything between us feels real to me. If you tell me that it doesn't feel that way to you, I won't bring it up again, and when we get back home, that'll be the end as planned. I promise I won't hound you like Mr. Ken Doll in there. And if you need to think about it, that's okay too." It wasn't fair of him to change the terms of their agreement and demand an answer immediately.

"You could never be as pigheaded as him. I'm not sure anyone could."

Dragging her teeth across her lips, she searched his face as her fingertips made a small circle against his arm. "When I asked for your help, I wasn't looking for a relationship. But almost from the beginning, this hasn't felt like an act. I think we should try being an actual couple." She shrugged a shoulder, and her mouth curved into a tentative smile. "And just see what happens."

ELEVEN

RATHER THAN VENTURE DOWNSTAIRS FOR BREAKFAST, TORY HAD suggested they either find a place away from the resort or stay in their suite. They certainly had enough food in the kitchen. She'd done so primarily because she enjoyed the time they spent alone getting to know each other or just talking about whatever came to mind. After this morning, they would only get a few chances to do that again until they returned to Boston. Although less of a factor, Grant had also played a role in her suggestion.

Last night he would've stood there all night if she hadn't walked away with Duncan. She'd boarded the plane yesterday aware there was a possibility Grant would want to talk. Still, she'd hoped that Duncan's presence would make him think twice before seeking her out. Throughout dinner, Tory had seen the looks Grant sent Duncan's way and crossed her fingers that he'd accept what was in front of him and leave her alone. Even when he'd called out to her near the elevators, she'd assumed the conversation would be short and put an end to anything further.

Unfortunately, she'd severely underestimated how pigheaded Grant could be. She'd noticed streaks of stubbornness in the past but never like last night. At some point before they left the island, he'd try to bend her to his will again—something that he'd never succeeded at, no matter how much pressure he put on her.

Although maybe she should thank Grant and his pigheadedness, though. During their conversation, she'd realized how right it felt to be with Duncan. Sure, she'd recognized the attraction she felt toward him long before her and Grant's little chat. But it hadn't been until he questioned if Duncan was right for her that she'd acknowledged their relationship felt natural and not like some act they were putting on for the benefit of others. Even so, she hadn't gone outside prepared to hear Duncan tell her that he felt the same way. And then he'd kissed her.

Unlike when she'd gone up to claim him, his lips had lingered against hers. She'd had her first boyfriend when she was fourteen, so she'd experienced plenty of kisses. And some had been more passionate, yet none had made her surroundings disappear and made her wish it would never end. Duncan's last night had done just that. Heaven help her if he'd turned up the intensity.

They'd shared a few more kisses while cuddling outside, discussing how they wanted to spend their free time this week. Eventually, they headed back to their suite and their separate bedrooms. This morning, Duncan had greeted her with a smile and a mocha latte from the café downstairs. Then, following a leisurely breakfast on the balcony, they got dressed and walked to the historical site next door.

But with that outing behind them and the time approaching noon, they couldn't put off meeting the rest of the wedding party any longer. If they did, Ivy would understand the reason behind their absences, but Preston wouldn't, since she'd specifically asked her friend not to discuss the situation between her and Grant with Preston.

And as soon as Duncan came downstairs, they'd head to the beach. Why he was taking so long was beyond her. They'd gone to their bedrooms at the same time to change. She'd finished twenty minutes ago and had been waiting on the balcony ever since.

"Sorry about that. My executive assistant called me, and I had to deal with a few matters." Duncan left a bottle of sunscreen on the table before joining her outside. He'd exchanged his khaki-colored shorts and golf-style shirt for swim trunks and a faded Boston Red Sox T-shirt.

"Believe me, I get it."

When she'd been growing up, business calls had been the norm for her dad, no matter where they were or what the family was doing. Even now, he was never fully away from work. Personally, she wanted work nowhere in sight when she was on vacation. But she understood some people were incapable of doing that and others weren't in a position to do it. She sensed it was a little of both in Duncan's case.

Compared to many other companies, his was still in its childhood. But if not for his and Matt's hard work, it never would've become the successful enterprise it was today. While everyone might not use Chat, a popular social media app, most people had heard of it.

"And I'm not complaining." There might not be sand between her toes, but her view was spectacular.

"Before I try to convince you we should stand your friends up, we should go."

Tory sighed and swung her legs off the lounge chair. "Trust me, it wouldn't take much effort." Now that they'd agreed this wasn't a charade, she could kiss him when she wanted. And now struck her as a perfect time.

"At least we can escape easily by going for a swim." She'd opted for her one-piece rather than her bikini for that very reason.

They had to wait longer than earlier for an elevator, but at least they had it to themselves when they stepped inside.

"What did you think of San Gerónimo?" Duncan asked as the elevator descended.

"I couldn't imagine living there. Could you?"

Duncan shrugged. "I guess it would depend on my alternatives. I'd make it work if it was there or on the street exposed to the elements. But if it came down to there or Versailles, it would be a different story."

"You've got a point." A lot came down to perspective. "Miguel was certainly passionate about the place."

The historical site didn't offer guided tours. Instead, visitors walked around the premises and read about the fort's history and how its occupants used its individual components and weapons on the information boards placed in various locations. However, a gentleman, obviously passionate about the island's history, greeted everyone when they entered. When Tory and Duncan arrived, they'd been the only ones there. Miguel had been more than happy to answer their questions. He'd shared with them far more information than posted on the official website or around the fortification. Before they'd gone off to explore the premises, he'd brought out a book containing photos, some of which dated back to the nineteenth century and were also not shown on the website Tory found.

"Yeah, it was clear how much he cared about the place. I think it's good to be passionate if you're going to work at a historical location like that."

The elevator stopped when it reached the sixth floor, and a couple holding hands joined them. Before the doors could fully close again, the last hotel guest she wanted to see approached them. It would've been inconsiderate, but if she'd been standing near the panel of buttons, she would've pressed the one to close the doors. But she wasn't the one closest to the panel; the taller of the two gentlemen who'd joined them was. Like a polite individual, he pressed the button to hold the doors open for Grant.

"Thank you," Grant said, stepping inside and nodding in the couple's direction.

Even though his destination was the same as theirs, it looked as if he'd spent hours working on his hair, and all she could think about was Duncan calling him Ken last night. And when Duncan squeezed her hand, she wondered if he had the same thought.

"What have you two been up to so far today?" Grant asked. "Everyone but you and Olivia met up for breakfast."

If there'd been a group breakfast, Ivy had not invited them, and Tory didn't think it'd been an accident.

"And we've all been down at the beach for a least the past hour. I just ran up to my room for my snorkeling stuff."

He wasn't being rude but making conversation, and if Drake or another groomsman had asked the same question, Tory wouldn't think twice about answering. The fact that the questions came from Grant simply rubbed her the wrong way. Especially after last night's conversation.

"We were busy doing other things."

At least to Tory, her tone suggested those things had been sexual, even though it was as far from the truth as a person could get. And judging by Grant's murderous expression, he'd interpreted her answer just as she'd hoped.

When the doors opened, the couple exited, still holding hands, and Tory and Duncan followed.

"We'll see you on the beach." It might be a little rude, but she wanted it clear to Grant that he wasn't welcome to walk with them.

The resort had set up all the cabanas in the same area, and at the moment, only three were in use, making it easy to find the group.

"Good, you're here. I was just about to text you." Ivy returned her cell phone to the beach bag near her seat. "Help yourself." She gestured toward the fruit and appetizers on the table. "The waitress just left, so if you want something other than water or hard seltzer, you'll have to go to the bar."

Duncan tossed the towels he carried on two empty beach chairs. "I'm going to get a mojito. Do you want anything?"

Hard seltzer was okay, but not what she was in the mood for

right now. The frozen concoction Ivy was sipping, though, looked yummy.

"A piña colada would be great."

"Grant, can I get you anything?" Duncan asked, being far more polite than she would've been if an ex-girlfriend of Duncan's was trying to come between them.

"I'm still trying to figure out what I want. I'll walk over with you and see what they have on the cocktail menu."

Duncan's expression didn't change, so she wasn't sure how he felt about Grant's statement. But it had Tory rethinking her answer. Maybe she should say she'd changed her mind and wanted to check out the menu too. If she walked over to the bar with them, her presence might deter Grant from saying something out of line to Duncan.

Gently squeezing her hand, Duncan gave her a kiss that fell somewhere between the polite one they'd exchanged at the auction and the toe-curling one he'd given her while outside last night.

"Be right back."

Tory watched her ex and her current boyfriend walk away and again considered going with Grant and Duncan.

He can take care of himself.

"I need to use the restroom. Come with me," Ivy said before she could sit down.

She recognized the accepted code women had used for generations when they wanted to talk privately and tossed the coverup she'd removed onto a chair.

The annoying sound of a hand dryer greeted Tory and Ivy when they walked inside. The things might cut down on waste and help the environment, but she hated them. She'd yet to use one that did a great job of drying her hands, and they were so darn loud, especially if more than one was in use like now.

Ivy waited until the two dryers stopped and they were alone to speak. "Either the two of you deserve an academy award, or you're no longer pretending to be together. So which is it?"

"No, we're not pretending. But how could you tell?"

Except for the kiss, they weren't acting any differently toward each other now than they had at dinner last night. At least, she didn't think they were.

"Let's start with the kiss you shared before he left to get drinks. My hair almost caught on fire just watching the two of you."

"You're exaggerating."

Ivy shook her head. "No, I'm not. There was something sensual about it. I can't explain it."

There was no point in arguing with Ivy. Tory rarely won when she did.

"Then we can move on to last night. The two of you were constantly touching each other."

Now that Ivy mentioned it, when Duncan hadn't been holding her hand, she'd had her fingers resting on his arm.

"I would've chalked it up to being part of your act, for Grant's sake, but I saw how you looked at each other. You're one of my closest friends, but your acting skills are not that good. So when did things change between you?"

"Officially, last night, but it's felt like we were together since almost the beginning."

"Aren't you glad you listened to me about bidding on someone at the auction? In another year, we might be at your and Duncan's wedding."

Following Ivy's advice brought Duncan into her life; how the relationship would ultimately turn out was anyone's guess. But Ivy was a die-hard romantic and wanted all her friends to have a happily ever after. A die-hard romantic wasn't the worst thing a person could be.

"You can safely hold off on buying me a wedding present just yet."

"Something tells me Duncan is Mr. Right."

"Yeah, well, can you send the memo to Grant? Because he didn't get it."

"Did he say something to you?"

"Last night after dinner." Opening the door, she waited for Ivy to exit before following behind her. "Brief version. He insisted we belong together."

"You came to a wedding with a boyfriend. How dense can he be?"

"Evidently, extremely." They walked by the children's pool and the line of guests waiting to get towels. "At least in his head, we didn't resolve the matter last night, either."

"Well, at least he hasn't been glued to your side. And Duncan won't stand for it if he tries."

DUNCAN HAD EXPERIENCED a lot of firsts in his life. Now he could add going to the bar with his girlfriend's ex to the list. It was a first he could've done without.

Four bartenders worked in the middle of the circular bar. Two of them focused on those guests using the stools built into the pool, while the other two filled the orders of the hotel guests waiting in line and those orders the waitstaff brought to them. Joining the line, Duncan remained silent. He hadn't believed Grant's line about not knowing what he wanted, but he couldn't stop the guy from walking with him either. But if he wanted to talk, Grant would have to start the conversation, because he had nothing to say to the man. At least, he didn't at the moment. If Grant continued to bother Tory like he had last night, he'd get involved.

Grant grabbed a cocktail menu off the bar and joined the line too. "So Tory said you have known each other since high school."

He didn't know where Grant was going with the conversation, but he'd be polite and answer. "Yeah, Tory was two years ahead of me at Philips."

"Lucky you. When I was a freshman, none of the older girls even looked my way."

Tory and Leah might have been the only female upperclassman he'd interacted with during his freshman year. And even then, it hadn't been often. Usually, it'd been a short conversation during a meal if Tory and Leah joined him and Alec, or when passing in the hallway.

"Her cousin Alec was my roommate. If he hadn't been, Tory and I probably wouldn't have been friends either."

"That makes more sense. I've met much of her family, but not her cousin Alec. Have you always lived in Boston?"

"No, I'm originally from New Hampshire. Most of my family lives there."

"Visited there once, and I couldn't wait to leave."

Funny, Duncan said the same thing about California.

"What can I get for you?" the bartender asked when it was their turn.

"A margarita with extra salt on the glass." Grant put the menu he'd never looked at on the bar. "And whatever he's having," he gestured toward Duncan.

"Thanks."

Maybe Grant was trying to be friendly. After all, they'd be spending a fair amount of time together over the next few days. Duncan doubted it though, not after last night. But for now, he'd let things play out and then go from there.

After giving the bartender his order, Duncan focused his attention on Grant. "You should think about visiting New Hampshire again. You might have just been in the wrong area."

"No, I've spent enough time in New England to know it's not for me. Tory surprised me when she told me she was moving there. It's not right for her either, at least not in the long term. The same goes for her new position. She'll get bored working for a regional magazine."

"People change. Tory seems very happy in Boston."

Tory's ex had known her for years, so Grant might know her better than Duncan. But at least in this area, he didn't think so.

Grant signed the receipt, charging the drinks to his room, and picked up his margarita. "I've known Tory my entire life. Living and working in Boston is just a phase. It wouldn't be the first one she's had."

He made Tory sound like a ditzy college student instead of a thirty-four-year-old professional.

"In another four to six months, she'll be ready to leave it all behind, including any new friends, and move back to California and either go back to working at the winery or for Trident."

Duncan sipped his drink as they walked around a pool and back onto the beach and considered the most polite way to tell Grant he thought he was full of shit. "You might be right, but I don't see her doing that."

"Benjamin and Shannon want her to be closer to them. Sometimes Tory rebels, but in the end, she always does what her parents want."

Yeah, that didn't sound at all like the Tory he'd gotten to know.

"That's initially how we got together earlier this year. Both our parents want to join the two families."

The last thing he wanted to hear about was Grant and Tory's relationship. "Then why isn't she here with you this week?" he asked before he thought better of it.

If Grant's goal was to make him jealous, he'd failed. Instead, he was annoying the hell out of him.

"Tory likes control, or at least the illusion that she's in control. Things between us got serious fast, and when she learned I planned to propose, she felt she was no longer in the driver's seat. Everything she's done since then has been her way of regaining control."

He disagreed. Tory liked to have a plan. The notebooks full of questions, so they knew as much about each other as possible, were a perfect example of that. But he wouldn't call her a control freak.

"But she knows as well as I do that it's just a matter of time before we're together. As I said, it's what our families and I want."

He'd met a lot of condescending jerks, but Mr. Ken Doll here beat them all. "What about Tory? Doesn't she get a say in any of this?"

"Deep down, it's what she wants too."

Even if theirs were a platonic relationship, similar to his and Alec's, Grant's comment would bother him.

"Tory told me she's not interested in being with you. Regardless of what you or her family want, you can't force her."

"There's something you need to know about Tory, Duncan. She'll use anyone to get the outcome she wants. Right now, she wants to have some fun and make me jealous. When she gets tired of you and life in Boston, she'll move back to California, and we'll pick up where we left off this summer."

He'd dealt with his share of people who'd use a person to get what they wanted and then split once they got it. He'd even dated some woman like that. But Tory didn't fit into that category.

"Listen, I'm telling you this as a friend. Don't get too invested in your relationship, because it won't last."

A whole host of words came to mind in response to Grant's statement. However, none of them would improve the situation, and he didn't want to start an argument. So instead, he lifted his drink higher.

"Thanks again for the drink. Next time they're on me," Duncan said before entering the cabana.

Accepting the glass, Tory kissed him. "I thought you got lost."

If Duncan brought up his and Grant's conversation, it would be when they were alone. "The bar was busy."

"I'm not surprised. It's a gorgeous day," Tory replied before removing the fruit added to her drink.

"After we finish these, are you up for renting a raft or going for a swim?"

Guests could rent single or double-person rafts to use on the ocean or in the pools on a first-come, first-serve basis. When he'd passed the hut where you obtained towels and rented them, there still had been some stacked outside. But if they waited much longer, they probably wouldn't get one today.

Tory removed the straw from her mouth and smiled. "I was going to suggest that myself."

TWELVE

Late Friday afternoon, Tory found Duncan outside on the balcony drinking iced tea and snacking on pretzels. "Have you been back long?"

After breakfast, Duncan had gone golfing with the men while she'd joined the women for a day of ultimate pampering at the resort's five-star spa. She was the most relaxed she'd been all month.

"We returned to the hotel about two hours ago, and then I went snorkeling for a little while. How was the spa?"

Duncan set down his drink, put his arm across her shoulders when she sat, and then kissed her temple. Whether it was holding her hand or putting an arm over her shoulders like now, Duncan liked physical contact—something she wasn't used to from past relationships but enjoyed.

"Just what I needed." She hadn't realized how tense her body was until today's massage. "I need to find a place at home that offers shiatsu massages." Before today, she'd never heard of that type, but there must be some place in Boston where she could get one.

"You got a massage too? That explains why you were gone

for so long. I thought you were just getting facials and having your nails done."

"Nope. Ivy wanted the works." In addition to the massages and manicures, they'd had facials and pedicures. "How was golfing?"

Although she'd expected Grant to seek her out again this week, he hadn't. He hadn't tried to speak to Duncan alone either. And even when the group was together, like yesterday during the distillery tour, Grant barely talked to either of them, which was fine with her. Hopefully, that meant he'd accepted they were never getting back together and he was ready to move on to someone else.

"Overall, it was a good day, although I thought about sticking a golf ball in Grant's mouth a few times. He acts like he's headed for the PGA tour and never stops pointing out what everyone is doing wrong. It'd be one thing if he were an outstanding player, but he's not. I'm better than him, and I'm only average on a good day."

"Yeah, that sounds about right. Grant's an expert at everything. We went skiing once, right after we started dating. After our third trail, I went inside the lodge and read while he skied for the rest of the afternoon."

"At least he didn't come to the bar with us after lunch. He claimed to have work to do. I think he was upset because Preston and Drake kept bringing up during lunch that he had the worst score of the day."

Going off to pout because the others were teasing him because he'd played poorly sounded like a Grant move. She didn't completely blame him either. No one liked to be reminded of their failures. But, at the same time, it was his own darn fault. If he didn't act like such a know-it-all, people wouldn't enjoy needling him so much when he lost.

"I wouldn't surprise me if Drake brings it up again tonight. Drake's not a fan of Grant and likes to get under his skin. He only tolerates him because Grant is Carrie's cousin."

"Yeah, I sensed they weren't best buds."

"Except for Preston and Steve, who is also Grant's cousin, he isn't friends with anyone else in the group. He often rubs people the wrong way."

Duncan's eyes widened in mock shock, and his jaw fell. "We must be talking about two different people. The Grant I know is such an easygoing, friendly person. I can't imagine him not getting along with everyone."

"I know, I know, it's hard to believe, but it's the truth," she said, playing along. "He has trouble making friends. Maybe you should offer to be his. You can go on golfing trips together or maybe visit Vegas. Grant loves poker. Don't worry if you're not great at the game. Grant would happily give you some pointers."

"Um, yeah, that's going to have to be a resounding no."

"Well, if you change your mind, I can give you his phone number," she said, patting his knee. "And as much as I'd love to stay out here with you, we need to get ready."

The wedding rehearsal and dinner weren't formal, but she couldn't wear what she had on. And Duncan definitely couldn't go in the bathing suit and faded Harvard T-shirt he had on right now.

"Do I need a tie?"

Standing, Tory extended her hand toward Duncan. "Not tonight, just tomorrow."

For Ivy and Preston's wedding rehearsal, the resort had roped off the portion of the beach where the ceremony would take place in the morning but had not bothered with anything else. But Ivy had shown her photos of what they had planned for the wedding, and it included hundreds of ocean-blue chairs, flowers along a white runner that would take the place of a center aisle, and a decorated ocean-blue pergola.

While she loved the beach, it wouldn't be her first choice for a wedding, especially this one. Unlike the beach at Cliff House, which was private and where more than one of her cousins had gotten married, here there was no way to prevent curious onlookers. Even tonight, hotel guests had paused throughout the rehearsal to see what was going on before continuing on their way. However, when Ivy had shared her and Preston's plans for a beach wedding, Tory wasn't surprised. The couple owned a home on the beach and usually only went on either beach vacations or cruises to exotic island locations.

"Do you want to run through everything one more time?" Jill, the wedding planner, asked.

When Ivy hired the planner, she said people waited months to book her. And after seeing Jill in action today, Tory didn't doubt it. The woman had everything running like a well-oiled machine, and if she ever got married and hired a wedding planner, Jill would be the first one Tory contacted.

"I don't think it's necessary. Preston, what do you think?" Ivy asked.

It was a wedding, not brain surgery, and they'd gone through it four times. If everyone didn't know what they needed to do by now, they never would.

"No, we're all set."

Thank goodness.

"Excellent." Jill checked the tablet in her hand. Why she bothered, Tory didn't know, because the woman probably had tonight and tomorrow's schedule memorized. "They should serve dinner in fifteen minutes."

Tomorrow's reception was in the resort's largest ballroom, but tonight's meal was being served outside. Like the spot on the beach, the resort had closed off the grassy area near some palm trees and set up tables as well as a buffet. Since there was enough room for dancing, Preston and Ivy had also hired a local DJ for the night. The same DJ would handle the music tomorrow. The original plan had been to have live music for the reception, but the couple could not agree on a band. Personally, Tory preferred a DJ for things like this, since it allowed for more variety in the songs played.

Her butt was inches from a chair when Tory caught sight of

the two couples walking toward the group of tables. Groaning, she lowered herself the rest of the way.

Since the bride and groom's parents had arrived earlier in the day, Tory expected to see them tonight. However, it hadn't occurred to her that Grant's parents would be there too, although it should've. Kenneth and Becky Castillo were not only Preston's aunt and uncle but also his godparents. The other couples' arrival explained why the hotel had set up more chairs than needed for the wedding party.

Rather than sit next to her, Duncan bent down toward her ear. "Something wrong?"

"Not really. I just didn't know Grant's parents would be here tonight too," she whispered.

"Which ones are his parents?" he asked, settling into the seat next to her.

"The couple on the left."

Duncan made a sound somewhere between a snort and a laugh. "Should've known by the hair."

Many men Kenneth Castillo's age had thinning hair, her father included, or no hair at all. Not Mr. Castillo. The man had hair many women would give their right arm to have. And much like his son, he put tremendous effort into his appearance.

"The couple walking with them is Preston's parents. And Ivy's mom and dad aren't far behind them."

The three approaching couples explained six of the extra chairs, but it still left four.

"Is Ivy's mother Gabriella Nelson from *Mornings with Gabriella and Lindsey*?" Duncan asked, referring to a popular morning talk show that had been on the air for at least twenty-five years.

"Yup. And Lindsey Hari is Ivy's aunt," she answered. "Lindsey and Gabriella are sisters."

"Really?" Duncan said, sounding surprised. "They don't resemble each other at all. I wonder if my mom knows they're sisters. She always enjoys watching the show."

As she listened to Duncan, Tory watched Ivy and Preston greet their most recent guests; then they escorted their parents to their table, leaving Grant with his parents.

After a brief conversation that included a few not-so-subtle looks in her and Duncan's direction, the three of them walked onto the grass.

Please don't sit here.

Ivy had assigned seats at tomorrow's reception but not for tonight's dinner. And at the moment, there were plenty of empty chairs at her and Duncan's table.

"So, who else is coming tonight?" Olivia asked as she pulled out a chair and sat.

She'd noticed Olivia had been trying to get close to Grant whenever the group was together. So far, it looked like she'd had little luck. If Grant sat with them, maybe Olivia could keep him occupied in a conversation.

"No idea," she answered, her eyes glued in Grant's direction. "I thought it would only be the wedding party tonight."

Just keep walking.

Either Duncan sensed the trio's ultimate destination, or he missed the physical contact, because he slipped his hand over hers moments before they reached the table. Although he'd touched her like this countless times this week, tingles once again shot up her arm, momentarily distracting her from the three people about to join them.

"Tory, I've missed you," Becky said, kissing Tory on the cheek, something she'd been doing for as long as Tory could remember. Then she moved to an empty chair and waited for her husband to pull it out before sitting—another thing Becky did all the time, at least when they were out in public.

"How have you been?" Becky asked.

Great. If Becky and Kenneth sat here, Grant would too.

"Fabulous. You?"

"I'm so glad to hear it, dear. Your mom has been worried about you. She'll be happy to hear you're doing so well."

Tory had told her mom numerous times since she moved that she was okay. If Mom refused to believe it, that wasn't Tory's fault or problem.

"I've been well. I returned from a vacation with my sisters two days ago. We went to Spain. They're still there. I would've stayed longer too, but we had Preston's wedding, and I didn't want to miss that."

Much like Tory's mom, it wasn't unusual for Becky to go on vacations without her husband. Those vacations were often with Shannon Sherbrooke, but Becky went with her sisters almost as often.

Before she could do the polite thing and make introductions, Grant did.

"Duncan, these are my parents," he said as he thankfully took the seat between Olivia and his mom instead of next to her. "Duncan is Tory's boyfriend." Although his voice remained unchanged, his pinched expression made him look like he'd bitten into a bitter lemon. It was not a good look for him.

It was good that she and Duncan were no longer acting, because before the weekend was over, her mom would know about their relationship, thanks to Grant's mom. Becky Castillo was a total sweetheart, the complete opposite of her husband, but she couldn't keep her mouth shut.

"A month or two ago, I read an article about you in *Business Leaders*. You and a college friend founded one of those silly social media apps seven or eight years ago," Grant's father said. The man had a monopoly on being blunt.

"Matt Sinclair and I founded Chat." If Kenneth's comment about Chat being a silly social media app bothered Duncan, she couldn't tell by his tone.

"I use Chat all the time," Hayden said as she and Gab got settled at the table.

Across the table, Olivia nodded. "Me too. I probably use it more than any of the other ones these days."

When Grant was around, you could always count on one

thing: He'd need to get his two cents in the conversation. Right now wasn't any different. "Social media is a necessary evil in today's world, including when it comes to business, Dad. I keep telling you that."

"Well, I'm glad we have sites like it. They make it so much easier to stay in contact with people," Becky said before moving the conversation onto a different topic.

DUNCAN WATCHED Grant's mom talking to her neighbor as he returned from the buffet table with two desserts. Mr. and Mrs. Castillo defied logic. Throughout dinner, Grant's mom had been friendly and had carried on conversations with everyone at the table, including him. Mr. Castillo had been the opposite. Much of the time, he remained silent, and when he spoke, it was to his son or, occasionally, his wife. The looks he'd sent toward Duncan, however, spoke volumes. Kenneth Castillo was possibly more upset than his son that Tory was no longer single.

Based on the little she'd told him, Duncan wondered if he'd get a similar reception from her dad. While they had no immediate plans with her family, he'd meet her parents eventually. With the holiday season approaching, it might even happen later this month or next.

Duncan hadn't mentioned it yet, but he hoped she'd join him and his family for Thanksgiving. He realized, though, it was possible she had plans. Thanksgiving was only six days away. He couldn't ask her to cancel on such short notice if she did.

"Duncan, Tory just mentioned you're originally from New Hampshire," Olivia said when Duncan rejoined the group.

Although they looked nothing alike, personality-wise Olivia reminded him a lot of his sister, and every time he saw her trying to get Grant's attention, he'd wanted to tell her Grant wasn't worth the effort. But, instead, he bit his tongue and hoped Tory or another friend would say something to her instead.

"What part?" she asked.

"I was born on Sanborn Island, but we moved to Windham when I was eleven." Since the late nineteenth century, Sanborn Island had been a favorite for society's elite, much like Martha's Vineyard, so she'd most likely heard of Sanborn. However, unless she'd lived in southern New Hampshire, he doubted she'd ever heard of Windham.

"My grandparents used to live in Portsmouth, and they had a vacation house in North Conway. When they sold both and moved to Florida, I bought the one in North Conway."

"Small world."

"Sometimes in the summer, we'd take the ferry over to Sanborn. I don't remember the name, but there was a place there that had the best homemade ice cream. We'd always stop when we were on the island."

"Sundae Scoops," Tory said before he could, because there was only one place she could be referring to. "Duncan and I spent last weekend on the island. We got ice cream because Duncan insisted it was better than anything I'd ever had. I hate to say he was right."

"I'm glad it's still open. It must be hard for small businesses to stay open on the island."

He was about to tell her that the business wasn't only still open, but it had expanded and now had shops in several New Hampshire towns, but he didn't get the chance.

"Duncan, have you ever thought about relocating Chat's headquarters?" Mr. Castillo asked out of the blue, moving the conversation about as far away from ice cream as it could get.

Duncan almost choked on the cake he'd swallowed. Except for his comment about the magazine article when he first sat down, Grant's father hadn't spoken directly to him all night. The man hadn't even asked him to pass the butter, which had been right in front of Duncan. Instead, he'd asked Hayden for it.

"Most big tech companies are in California," Mr. Castillo continued before Duncan answered.

The fact that most companies like theirs were in California was just one reason Duncan and Matt preferred to remain in New England. However, the primary reason behind the location they'd picked was because of its proximity to family. Most of Matt's family lived in western Massachusetts or Vermont, while much of Duncan's remained in New Hampshire.

"No. Matt and I both enjoy living in New England, and it's home for most of our family members."

"Staying in a location because it's close to family isn't a sound business decision," Mr. Castillo said. "You should reconsider. All the best talent is in California. I have a lot of connections and could help you find a better location."

Go to hell. "I appreciate the advice and the offer, and I'll keep both in mind."

"Must be nice having your family all in one area. I think mine tried to get as far away from each other as possible," Hayden said with a little laugh.

"My cousin CJ lived in California for about sixteen years, but he moved back a year ago. And my sister did an internship in DC, but she accepted a position working on Congressman Joel Seabrook's campaign and moved back to New Hampshire in January." She'd only moved out of their parents' house again in July, and he still wasn't sure who was happier about that, his mom or Harper. Although since the congressman had lost his reelection bid earlier this month, his sister would soon be out of a job. And that might mean she moved back in with their parents.

Tory's hand stopped with her fork almost to her mouth, and she gave him a look he couldn't even begin to decipher before she put the fork down and picked up her drink instead.

"What a minute. Is CJ Ferguson your cousin?" Olivia asked.

He never went out of his way to tell people CJ Ferguson was his cousin. However, if people asked, he never denied it either.

"Yeah, our fathers are brothers."

"He's one of my favorite actors. I think I've seen all his

movies. Is he going to be in anything new soon? It's been over a year since a movie came out with him in it. And I have read nothing about him in ages. He used to be on the cover of a different magazine every week."

Since getting married, CJ had been keeping a low profile and living in North Salem, a small town on the North Shore of Massachusetts. However, he and his wife had spent most of the summer on Sanborn Island and planned to return for Thanksgiving.

"CJ has one project coming up, but I don't know the specifics."

Honestly, Duncan knew everything about it, including when filming started and who else would be in the film, but he wasn't at liberty to share.

"I know he married a high school history teacher. Are they still together?"

Olivia's question made sense. Celebrity marriages weren't known for their longevity.

"Yeah, CJ and Isabelle are still together." He didn't see that changing either. Although they'd gone their separate ways for over a decade, CJ had loved Isabelle since high school.

The instrumental background music stopped, and a popular love ballad he couldn't stand and always switched off when it came on replaced it. Hayden and Gab, as well as Drake and Carrie at the table next to them, interpreted that to mean the dance floor was open for the evening.

"Do you want to dance, Grant?" Olivia asked as she pushed her empty dessert plate away from her.

Grant looked at Tory and glared at Duncan before answering. "Sure."

Standing, Mr. Castillo pulled back his wife's chair. "Grant, your mother and I are going to head to our suite. We'll see you in the morning."

Nice job asking your wife what she wants to do. Damn,

Grant's father was an ass. It was no wonder his son had turned out to be one too.

"Duncan, it was a pleasure meeting you. I'll see you both at the wedding." Once again, Mrs. Castillo kissed Tory's cheek before slipping her purse over her shoulder.

Somehow, it didn't surprise him when Mr. Castillo walked away without even a simple goodbye to either of them.

"I see where Grant gets his winning personality from."

He dealt with rude people all the time. Unfortunately, it was a part of life. But Tory's father and Mr. Castillo were close friends, or so Tory claimed. You'd think the guy would be polite to his friend's only daughter. The one that you wanted to marry your son and become part of your family.

Tory took another bite of her dessert, and her lips closed around the fork. Although his mind shouldn't be going there, he envisioned her lips doing the same thing, only around him.

Don't go there.

"What do you think of the dessert?" he asked as a way to clear the erotic images from his head.

He didn't know the name of it, but it had looked tasty, so he'd selected it for her. He wasn't sure what his dessert was called or what was in it either, but it was delicious. Currently, he was contemplating a second piece while there was still some left.

"It's excellent. You made a great selection. Yours?"

"Great. I wish I knew what it's called." Without knowing what it was, it'd be almost impossible to look for at home. "So, is Mr. Castillo always so friendly?"

Tory took another forkful before answering. "He's never as friendly as Becky, but he is usually better than he was tonight. Kenneth wasn't happy you were with me."

"Really? I hadn't noticed." Duncan added an extra dose of sarcasm to his voice. "I thought he was going to offer to adopt me."

The dimple he always wanted to kiss when he saw it

appeared, and she touched his forearm. "Don't worry. I'm happy you are here." Leaning closer, she kissed his cheek.

"How about you try that again?" He turned in his chair so that he faced her.

Tory's smile grew, and she skated her lips against his. The act was soft and sweet. "Believe me, I'm delighted you are here."

She pressed her lips against his again. This time, the kiss was anything but sweet. Everyone and everything slipped away as heat coursed through his body and all his blood headed south below his belt. Not exactly the best place for it to be at the moment. Unfortunately, he was powerless to stop it.

Tory broke away, a small smile still on her face. "Convinced now?"

"Yeah, I'd say so."

"Good. Do you want to dance?"

She'd know what he wanted if she looked down, and it wasn't dancing. Their relationship had yet to go past kissing. Mentally, he had no issues with that. Even if you counted the time they'd spent together before landing in Puerto Rico as the start of their relationship, they hadn't been together long. He'd slept with a few women after only a few dates, but unlike some of his friends, he preferred to know a woman well before becoming intimate. At least for him, it added to the experience. He assumed Tory felt the same because she'd never tried to move things into the bedroom.

Unfortunately, his body wasn't always on the same page, like now.

Dancing was one of those things he could take or leave. But she wouldn't have asked if she didn't want to dance. "Sure, but let's finish dessert first."

Maybe by then, his body would've forgotten about their kiss.

Yeah, right.

THIRTEEN

HEARING THAT HARPER, DUNCAN'S YOUNGER SISTER, HAD completed an internship in Washington, DC, and now worked for Congressman Joel Seabrook had caught her off guard. Not once had Duncan mentioned his sister or any member of his family was interested in politics. Of course, she hadn't asked either, but it wasn't a topic that often came up in conversation. However, outside, she'd quickly dismissed the information because not everyone who worked for a politician or spent time in DC wanted to hold an office someday. Instead, many wanted to work as speech writers or be a part of the politician's public affairs team.

Suspicion crept its way back into her head on their way upstairs, and she'd been unable to shove it aside again. And then, while sitting on the balcony, she'd brought up the subject. Now, as she stared toward the ceiling—the room was so dark she couldn't see it—she wished she hadn't.

According to Duncan, his sister planned to run for a seat in the New Hampshire House of Representatives next year. Then possibly move on to a seat in Congress once she had experience and had reached the minimum age required. However, he'd admitted that he didn't understand why his sister would want to enter either local or national politics. His actual words had been that he'd prefer to work cleaning rest stop bathroom toilets with a toothbrush than work on Capitol Hill.

On that, Tory agreed. How so many of her family members did it was the equivalent of the Bermuda Triangle in her book.

Duncan's personal view, though, did nothing to dismiss the suspicion nagging at her. Even in a local election, the Sherbrooke name would go a long way. Duncan loved his sister, but would he get involved with Tory in the hopes it would give his sister a significant boost?

The night of the auction, she'd proposed the crazy idea of him pretending to be her boyfriend, and he had agreed quickly. But at the same time, he had no way of knowing their relationship would change. Everything could have played out as they'd agreed, and on Sunday, when they landed in Boston, they would go their separate ways.

Or everything he'd said to her their first night here could have been part of a plan—one designed to end the charade and make their relationship real so his sister, and possibly even his company, could reap the benefits.

"You're overthinking this," she said. "Duncan doesn't have an ulterior motive. He's not Grant or Luke."

She didn't think of her ex-fiancé often, but he popped into her thoughts now. When they'd first met, she hadn't known that Luke had any political aspirations. Even when he'd proposed six months after their first date, she still hadn't known that he planned to run for Congressman Russ Crowley's seat the following year when the congressman retired. She hadn't learned of Luke's intent until she'd overheard him talking to his dad at a party. That night she'd been about to walk away rather than eavesdrop when she heard her name. After that, she'd been unable leave. Instead, she'd listened as Luke explained how his connection to the Sherbrooke family after their marriage would all but ensure he won the election.

"Duncan is nothing like Luke," she repeated.

Turning onto her side, she punched her pillow. If she didn't get some sleep, she'd look like hell in the morning. And she'd prefer not to resemble a raccoon in Ivy's wedding photos.

The cell phone on the nightstand rang, as if the universe had something against her sleeping. Tory didn't need to look to know the call was from one of two people. Ever since the Castillos returned to their hotel room, she'd known a call from either Mom or Dad was imminent. But when ten o'clock came and went, she'd assumed it wouldn't come until tomorrow.

A glance at the phone confirmed her assumption. Either Mom had forgotten about the time difference between California and Puerto Rico because she never called this late—or early, depending on how you looked at it—or there had been a family emergency.

"Why didn't you tell me you were seeing someone?" Mom asked after greeting Tory.

Grateful the call wasn't because of an emergency, Tory switched on the bedside lamp and sat up. Some conversations required an upright position. This was one of them.

"Instead, I had to learn about it from Becky. Do you have any idea how embarrassing that was? A mother should know what's going on in her daughter's life. And that includes a vacation with a man I've never met and didn't even know was in your life."

Rolling her eyes, Tory waited for a break in her mom's lecture and, not for the first time in her life, wished she had parents more like her cousin Leah's or any of the cousins on that branch of the Sherbrooke family tree.

"I didn't think of it." At one in the morning, it was the best lie she could come up with.

"You didn't think of it." Somehow, the volume of Mom's voice never changed, but her outrage still came through loud and clear. "What kind of excuse is that?"

"Mom, it's one o'clock, and I have to be at the salon at six to get my hair and makeup done for Ivy's wedding. Can we talk about this later?"

She already knew the answer, but she asked the question anyway because she might get lucky. Mom liked Ivy, and she would want Tory looking her best for the wedding.

"No, we cannot."

It was never a good sign when Mom didn't use contractions in a conversation.

"You can have extra coffee if you're tired, and makeup does wonders for covering circles under the eyes."

Yup, just the answer she'd expected.

"If you're on vacation with someone, I at least need to know who he is. How long have you even known him? You've been in Boston less than a month."

Tory took a deep breath as she counted to three. "We didn't just meet, Mom," she said and then launched into their predetermined story. She also threw in that Duncan and Alec were close friends for good measure.

"Well, if he's a friend of Alec's, it makes me feel a little better."

Tory didn't need Mom to explain her comment.

"But what about Grant?"

"I don't see what Grant has to do with Duncan and me."

"You and Grant are perfect for each other."

Wow, had Grant recently gotten together with her parents and come up with that line?

"Many couples go through a separation period," Mom continued.

To say many couples went through such a period was an exaggeration but not entirely untrue.

"If you give him another chance, I'm confident you can work things out, Tory."

Maybe she should record her response, so every time they had this conversation, she could play it while she went and did something else.

"Mom, we've gone over this. Everyone is wrong. Grant and I are not right for each other. You and Dad, Grant, and his parents need to accept that."

"On that we'll have to agree to disagree."

There was no point in pressing the issue. No matter what Tory said, Mom wouldn't change her mind. "Fine, Mom."

"In about two weeks, we'll be in the Boston area. We'll get together then so we can meet Duncan."

Her parents didn't travel to the East Coast often, and she wondered why they were coming now. But, while she was curious why they were headed her way, she didn't care enough to inquire tonight. Monday or Tuesday would be soon enough.

"Okay, just let me know the date, and I'll talk to Duncan. Now can I go? It's late here." Or early.

Either way, she wanted to go to sleep.

"I suppose so." Mom's tone said it all. She wanted to press the matter but recognized the wedding was hours away. "Say hello to Preston and Ivy for me and give them my best."

WHEN IVY and Preston had planned their big day, they'd kept the traditional parts of a wedding they liked and ditched the rest. Overall, she agreed with most of their decisions, especially getting rid of a head table where the entire wedding party sat together at the reception. It didn't get much more awkward than sitting in front of the room and eating while everyone gawked at you. She didn't have an opinion on the speeches by the best man and maid of honor. She'd never had an issue with speaking in front of groups. But she knew having them had been part of a compromise. Preston had wanted to include them but skip the throwing of the bouquet and the cake cutting, while Ivy had wanted all three. In the end, they kept the speeches and the cake cutting but skipped the tossing of the bouquet.

One tradition Tory wished they'd nixed was the wedding

party dance. Unfortunately, the couple agreed on that one, and once Preston and Ivy finished their first dance, as maid of honor, she'd have to take the dance floor with Grant, her counterpart.

"At this time, the bride and groom would like the wedding party to join them on the dance floor," the DJ said when the music stopped.

"Unfortunately, that's your cue," Duncan whispered when she didn't move.

She saw Grant walking toward her rather than the dance floor. Ivy had put Grant and his parents at a table with one of Preston's other uncles.

"Don't remind me." Tory tossed her napkin on the table.

"Maybe you should take that with you. You can stick it in Grant's mouth if he talks." Before she stood, Duncan brushed his lips across her bare shoulder, setting off a cascade of tiny explosions.

Beside her chair, Grant cleared his throat, and she ground her teeth together.

"Everyone is waiting for us."

Two of the required five couples had joined Ivy and Preston, so they weren't the only ones missing. But she wouldn't argue and cause a scene. Instead, she kissed Duncan and pushed back her chair. "Be back as soon as I can."

Last night on the dance floor, her body had unconsciously leaned into Duncan when he put his arms around her. Now the opposite happened, and Tory stepped back, forcing more distance between her and Grant.

"How was your week?" Grant asked as a slow ballad started and he moved closer, swallowing up some of the space she'd made.

She could handle a conversation about her week if they had to talk. "Wonderful. Yours?"

"It could've been better."

"Unfortunately, that happens sometimes."

"You're not going to ask me why?" Grant asked, sounding mildly annoyed.

Why ask the question when one, she didn't care, and two, she already knew the answer he'd give her?

"No. I assumed if you wanted to tell me, you would."

Grant made a sound in the back of his throat and moved them to the left. "Are you leaving tomorrow or staying a few more days? I'm staying until Monday and then heading to Hartford for two days."

Where are you going with this conversation?

"Duncan and I are leaving in the early afternoon."

Grant guided them even farther away from the other couples as he spoke. "Have you considered that Duncan might be more interested in your last name than you?"

Oh, like you?

He didn't pause long enough for her to say it.

"His company is still fairly new, and clearly his sister has political aspirations."

If walking away and leaving Grant standing there alone wouldn't cause a scene, she'd do it in a heartbeat.

"I think you're confusing Duncan with yourself."

The muscle in his jaw twitched. "You'll see I'm right about Duncan and us."

Rather than take the bait, she imagined herself sticking her napkin in his mouth and remained silent until the music ended.

"Have a safe trip home, Grant. Oh, and have a pleasant holiday." She walked away before Grant could escort her back to her seat.

EARLY THIS MORNING, they'd shared a quick breakfast, which she'd yawned her way through. It had annoyed him when Tory told him what time her mom had called last night. But he'd been angry when he learned Shannon Sherbrooke had refused to wait until a more decent hour to chat. His mom wasn't perfect, but she respected his boundaries. It sounded like Tory's mom could use a few lessons from his mother.

After she left for the salon, Duncan went to the beach to pass the time. And the next time he'd seen Tory, she'd been walking down the makeshift aisle, looking more beautiful than the bride. Traditional wedding party photos followed before she finally joined him in the ballroom for lunch. Throughout the meal, she'd been quieter than she usually was when they were together. But he chalked it up to her being tired.

Then that damn antiquated wedding party dance took place. In all fairness, Duncan had taken part in them, and they'd never bothered him. And if Tory had danced with a different groomsman, he would've tolerated it far better. But seeing Grant's hand on her waist brought out the caveman inside him. He'd wanted to walk onto the dance floor, punch Grant in his smug face—because although he couldn't hear their conversation, he doubted it was one Tory wished to have—and then mess up Grant's perfect hair *just because* before taking Tory in his arms and finishing the dance.

While he'd done all four in his mind, his ass had stayed glued to his seat as he listened to Gab, Tory's former coworker and Hayden's boyfriend, talk about wine. Duncan had never met anyone so enthusiastic about it.

When Tory returned, she had shared nothing about her conversation with Grant, and he hadn't asked. Instead, she ordered another coffee and listened to Gab while the bride and groom each had their dances with their parents.

Eventually, Hayden wrangled the conversation away from wine and onto the upcoming holidays. Despite the new topic, Tory remained quiet, only occasionally adding anything. Again, he attributed her lack of participation to her being tired.

However, he couldn't blame the change in her since sitting down on her lack of sleep. It was a subtle change but there. Before, she was quiet but still engaged in her surroundings. Now she was aloof, as if lost in her thoughts. Grant had to be the cause, but until they were alone, he couldn't ask her.

"You seem tired. Do you want to call it a day?" Honestly, it looked like she was struggling to keep her eyes open.

Tory moved her hand off his shoulder and covered yet another yawn. "I'm way past tired. Let's finish this dance, then go and stop at the café and grab an espresso on the way. Then maybe we can change and go down to the pool."

It'd been a morning wedding, so it was only midafternoon. Still, Duncan thought she'd be better off getting an hour of sleep than espresso before going down to the pool, but what did he know?

"Whatever you want." As long as he didn't have to interact with Grant, he was open to anything.

Even after the song ended and they exited the dance floor, it took several minutes to leave the ballroom. Understandably, Tory wanted to say goodbye to the bride and groom and her other friends before she left. However, it didn't escape Duncan that she didn't stop by the Castillos' table.

A long line, considering the time of day, greeted them at the café, but eventually, they made it up to their suite. The entire time, he'd carried on a one-sided conversation. Now, though, as they looked for two seats together by the pool, she was once again herself.

"Ivy and Preston's wedding fit the couple to a T. It was what I would've planned for them if they'd asked me to."

"It wasn't what I'd want, but it was nice." Duncan stopped by two empty chairs. "How about these?"

While not right by the main pool, they were a short walk to it and the hot tubs. The bar wasn't far from the spot, either. Even better, there were no children around them. He had nothing against children; he just didn't want them running around him right now.

Tory tossed a towel on one and then kicked off her flip-flops.

"Some of my cousins have had more traditional church weddings. But I think an outdoor wedding can be beautiful."

"I was referring to the size, not the location. Even if Ivy and Preston both have large families, those couldn't have all been relatives, not unless they invited everyone up to their tenth cousin once removed."

"They both have big families, but not everyone there was a relative. Some were friends, and others were people they felt they had to invite, like Mr. Nelson's business partners. Obviously, you've never been to a Sherbrooke wedding, because this was smaller than some of my cousins'."

It would be his first when Alec and Gianna married, but he imagined they were often huge.

"Callie and Dylan's wedding was by far the largest. And Brett and Jennifer's this summer was almost as big. The smallest was Jake and Charlie's, but they had a secret wedding in Hawaii and invited only a handful of people."

"It wouldn't shock me if Gianna suggested she and Alec have a smaller wedding."

Smaller, of course, being a relative term, since Alec was one of five and all his siblings were married. Not to mention, his friend considered many of his cousins to be more like siblings.

"Has Gianna said anything to you about when the wedding will be?"

Duncan shook his head. They had yet to discuss it, but he had a good idea when it wouldn't take place. "If we were placing bets on when it will be, I'd say sometime in the winter or early spring. Gianna won't want it to coincide with May Point's busy season."

"Haven't you learned your lesson about betting? It was a bet that earned you a spot at the auction."

He'd hated every second of being on stage, but the event had brought them together—something that might not have happened otherwise, so he wouldn't complain. "Hey, I didn't say we should bet on when it will be, just that if we did."

"Your cousin would not get married in the summer because of work?"

"She's under the assumption the company would go under if she's not around. I think she forgot Uncle Corey ran it for years and could take her place for a week or two."

"She sounds a little like my dad. He's never really on vacation. Dad is just away from the office, if you know what I mean," she said before giving her drink order to the server who'd stopped by them.

Duncan was familiar with the type. He'd been much the same way when he and Matt started Chat. Over the past year or two, he'd been trying to have a life again, because you only got one.

Tory waited until he ordered a drink too before speaking again. "Mom and Dad are visiting in a few weeks. I'm sure he'll spend at least half the trip on his phone or laptop. While they're here, they want the four of us to get together so they can meet you."

He had several things on his calendar between Thanksgiving and the week before Christmas because he'd originally planned to spend Christmas week through New Year's on Sanborn Island. But he'd find a way to squeeze time in to meet Tory's parents if that was what she wanted.

"I'll be there. Just give me a day, time, and place."

"Mom didn't say when they'd be around. And since it was one in the morning, I didn't ask. Next time we talk, I'll get more details. I'm sure she'll call me this week, considering how our conversation ended this morning."

If she wanted him to meet her parents already, Tory might be open to meeting his family.

"Do you have plans for Thanksgiving?"

"Not exactly. Scott and Paige invited me to join them, but I declined because I didn't feel like going to New York. And Callie and Dylan asked me to come to their house, but since Warren will be there, so will the Secret Service. I don't want to deal with them. But Judith, Leah's mom, asked me to join them on Saturday. That's when they're celebrating Thanksgiving this year. Leah's stepdaughter won't be with Leah and Gavin until then. Judith considers Erin her granddaughter and doesn't want to celebrate without her."

He'd never met Alec's aunt Judith, but he liked her already.

"Why?" she asked.

"I'm going to my aunt and uncle's house. The aunt you met last weekend. I'd like you to come with me."

"She won't mind an extra person?"

"Aunt Audrey will wonder where you are if you don't come. My parents will be there too. Maybe Gianna and Alec. I don't know what their plans are."

Tory accepted the fruity cocktail she'd ordered from the server and signed the receipt, charging both drinks to the room. "Then count me in. Are you free to come with me on Saturday?"

He didn't need to check his calendar to know his only plans for the weekend involved eating and seeing family.

"I think I can tear myself away from eating leftovers long enough to come." There was nothing quite like leftover turkey and stuffing sandwiches. "Who else will be there?" he asked before taking a sip of his margarita and placing it on the table between them.

Frowning, she put her cup down with more force than necessary, and he was glad it was made plastic and not glass. "Why does it matter?"

He hadn't expected her reaction. "It doesn't." Duncan couldn't think of any reason his innocent question would bother her, but it clearly did.

"Then why did you ask?"

"I was just wondering if I'd know anyone there." Over the years, he'd meet some of Alec's relatives but not all of them.

"Sorry." She shook her head as if to clear it. "That came out the wrong way. Leah and her brothers will be there with their families. Marilyn and Harrison will be there too. Marilyn is Jonathan's sister."

"I met Alec's aunt and uncle at a Fourth of July party his dad and stepmom had. Alec's uncle was still a senator, so it was a while ago. I've never met Leah's brothers."

"You'll get along with Brett and Curt. Leah's husband, Gavin, too."

"I look forward to meeting them."

Tory's lips curved into a slight frown again.

Now what did I say?

"Will we leave for Sanborn Island on Wednesday night?" she asked, rather than explain her displeasure.

"Early Wednesday afternoon, if we can. We can come back either Friday afternoon or Saturday morning. Up to you."

"We don't need to decide right now. I don't remember what time dinner is at Jonathan's anyway."

He might regret what he was about to say. "Is something wrong? You've been off ever since your dance with Grant."

"Nope, everything is fine," she answered, not quite meeting his gaze. "Listening to Grant tell me how perfect we are for each other with only three hours of sleep just got on my nerves. Thankfully, I won't see him again anytime soon now that the wedding is over and we're leaving tomorrow."

It would get on his nerves, too, if he had to listen to Grant talk about anything, regardless of how much sleep he'd had the previous night. But he got the impression there was more behind Tory's mood today. But if she didn't want to share, he wouldn't push the matter. When she was ready, she'd tell him.

FOURTEEN

"WHAT DID I MISS?" GIANNA ASKED, FOLLOWING HIM INTO THE room.

Duncan added his and Tory's jackets to the pile on the bed in the guest bedroom. The same room Gianna had called her own for years.

"You're going to have to be more specific, Gi." They hadn't spoken in at least two weeks. And since he and Tory ended up not visiting when they'd been on the island, Duncan hadn't seen his cousin since the auction.

"I found Tory in the kitchen with my mom. You told me you were helping her out by going to Puerto Rico as her boyfriend. That was last week, so why is she here with you now?"

He'd always considered Gianna more than a cousin. She was more like a sister and good friend, all rolled into one. She knew him better than anyone, including Alec, and he considered Alec his best friend. He usually shared any significant changes in his life with her, including when he got into a new relationship. Duncan had intended to call Gianna this week so Tory's presence wouldn't surprise her or Alec, but he'd never gotten around to it. He thought Aunt Audrey would've said something to Gianna after he sent her a text message letting her know he was bringing a guest. Evidently, either she hadn't, or she'd failed to share a name with her daughter. Although it didn't matter, he wanted to know which it was.

"Your mom didn't tell you Tory was coming?"

"Last night, she mentioned you were bringing a girlfriend. I was going to call and ask what was up, but Alec distracted me. Afterward, it was too late."

Duncan didn't need Gianna to elaborate on how Alec had distracted her. The slight blush did it for her.

"I don't believe for a second that she had nowhere else to go. Her parents aren't local, but she has plenty of relatives nearby that I'm sure invited her to join them."

Yep, Gianna was right. Tory could've gone somewhere else today.

"She's here because I invited her."

"Well, duh. I guessed that already, Einstein. So does that mean you're no longer pretending, or did you ask her here as a friend?"

It might be childish, but he enjoyed annoying Gianna too much to pass up a great opportunity like this. "What do you think?"

"I think you're intentionally being difficult." Gianna crossed her arms and glared at him. "Out with it, or I'm not inviting you to the wedding."

Duncan shrugged. "Well, Alec will, so I'm not worried about it. Speaking of the wedding, have you decided on a date?"

"Answer my question first, and then I'll answer yours."

Duncan intended to answer her anyway. "Things between us changed while in Puerto Rico, so to answer your question, we're no longer pretending." Actually, the relationship had started to change for him even before they even came to the island the first time.

"When you brought her here before your trip, I had a feeling that would happen. You rarely bring anyone you're with here. The last woman you did was Willow, I think."

He'd prefer not to be reminded of Willow, the gold-digging witch. But his cousin was correct. Willow was the last woman he'd been involved with that he'd brought to Sanborn and introduced to his family.

"I'm happy for you. I haven't spent much time with Tory, but she seems nice," Gianna continued.

Duncan intended to fix that. He wanted the woman he was falling in love with and his favorite cousins to be friends.

"Good, you didn't get abducted by aliens," Alec said when Duncan and Gianna joined him downstairs.

"Your much better half was interrogating me. Gi threatened to leave me off the guest list for the wedding if I didn't comply."

Alec put his arm around his fiancée's waist. "I would've sent you an invitation anyway."

"That's what I told her, but I answered her questions anyway. She gave me that evil stare of hers."

"I'm familiar with it," Alec said, his comment earning him an elbow to the stomach.

"You deserved it, Alec," Tory said, joining them. "Your aunt poured this for you." She held out a cup of steaming spiced apple cider. He didn't know what she put in it. However, she always had it on hand during the holidays, and he always looked forward to it.

"I was going to wait until after dinner, but since we're talking about the wedding, I'll ask you now. Duncan, will you be my best man?"

Duncan had expected to be in the wedding but not as the best man. Alec had three older brothers and more male cousins than he could recall at the moment. He hoped Alec wasn't asking because Gianna was his cousin.

"Definitely."

"Don't worry, Alec didn't ask because you're my cousin," Gianna said, as if she could read his mind. "I know how he thinks, Tory. Call me if you ever need someone to help you figure him out."

He wished he could contradict her, but he couldn't. Gianna had always been able to read him and know when something bothered him. It was a skill he had as well, where she was concerned.

EVERY YEAR TORY CELEBRATED THANKSGIVING. Sometimes dinner was at her parents' home. Other years, she joined an aunt and uncle for the day. And when she'd been rooming with Leah in high school, she'd gone to Jonathan and Judith's home in Weston, Massachusetts. But none of those celebrations resembled this one.

To start, regardless of the house, family members didn't arrive carrying pies, trays of cookies, or extra sides. Tory never chatted with Mom or whichever aunt was hosting while she prepared the meal. Instead, either the family's chef cooked the turkey and all the sides or the family had them catered. Desserts were ordered or prepared by the family cook.

The differences didn't stop with the food, though. When Tory's mom hosted, everyone gathered at the mile-long table in the exquisitely decorated dining room. Okay, that was an exaggeration, but everyone sat together in the same room.

Not here. Eight of Duncan's relatives sat squeezed together around a table designed for six people. While the dining room was lovely and filled with items that reflected the family, photos of it would never find their way into *Boston Home, Life, and Style*. Another six people sat in folding chairs at a table set up in the living room while the last four guests ate in the kitchen.

She couldn't hear every conversation, but the ones at her table covered every topic under the sun. That was how she knew Duncan's cousin CJ was having dinner with his wife's family, but they would be by later for dessert. She'd also learned that CJ's younger sister Brianna had remained in California for the holiday but should be home for Christmas.

"Can I have the potatoes when you're done with them?" Tory asked.

Gianna added a heaping spoonful of mashed potatoes to her plate and then passed the bowl across the table. "Are you all settled yet?"

"More or less. There is still a little decorating I want to do, but I'm all unpacked. Alec, didn't you ever hear of something called color?"

The same off-white paint covered every room in the condo. It was the same way in Duncan's condo, or at least in the rooms she'd seen. She assumed the off-white paint was standard in the building. She didn't need her place to look like a crayon box exploded, but she wanted a little variety.

Alec accepted the sweet potato casserole from Duncan, although Tory didn't know where he planned to put it. His plate was already full.

"White is a color."

"It's fine in one or two rooms but not everywhere."

"I'm just giving you a hard time. I planned to change things when I bought the condo but never got around to it."

"Where did you live before you moved, Tory?" Harper asked.

Duncan's sister looked like a younger version of their mother, only with lighter hair. Like everyone Tory had met today, Harper had been welcoming.

"Northern California."

"I'm guessing you moved for work, because I can't think of one good reason to move to Boston."

Tory nodded as she scooped up a forkful of the sweet potato casserole, a dish she'd never tried, but Duncan had gone on and on about how delicious his aunt's recipe was. "I started working for *Boston Home, Life, and Style Magazine* in October. You're not a fan of the city?" The more time she spent there, the more she liked Boston.

"Boston is okay for a few hours, but I wouldn't want to live there. There is something about it that is just off. I can't explain it. I much prefer New York City or DC. Did you work for a magazine before, too, or did you work for Sherbrooke Enterprises?"

"Neither. I worked for Desjardin Winery."

"I've had wine from there. Going from a winery to a magazine seems like an unusual change."

"My first job after college was at Trident Corporation, which my grandfather started and my family still owns. From there, I went to Desjardin, which my father owns. For once, I wanted to work somewhere that wasn't connected to my family."

"I didn't know the Sherbrookes owned Desjardin," Harper said.

A lot of people didn't. "My dad bought the winery from my mom's family about forty years ago. He wanted nothing to do with Sherbrooke Enterprises or hotels, and my dad wasn't satisfied with his limited role at Trident. My grandfather was a bit of a control freak and waited as long as he could to turn things over to his children."

Even now, her grandfather visited Trident's headquarters at least once a month and insisted on meetings with her uncles and cousins who worked there.

"The only hotels I'd want to worry about are the ones on a Monopoly board, so I don't blame Benjamin," Alec said as he raised a fork toward his mouth.

"You don't work for Sherbrooke Enterprises either?" Harper asked, sounding surprised.

"Not directly. I started working for the Helping Hands Foundation this summer. It's one of Sherbrooke Enterprises charitable foundations."

"Thanks for the reminder, Alec. How was the auction? I asked Duncan to get me a ticket, but he refused."

"Hey, you could've bought your own," Duncan replied.

"The tickets were a little out of my price range. And you could've been a nice big brother and paid for at least half. The only reason you refused was because you were in it. If CJ had been the one getting auctioned off, you would've bought everyone in the family a ticket, and you know it."

"She's right, Duncan," Gianna said. "Don't worry, Harper; Alec recorded it. I'll send it to you."

Tory listened as Gianna shared all the details from the auction with her younger cousin. Every once in a while, Alec added something. Eventually, Duncan got them to move on to a new topic. She didn't blame him for not wanting to discuss the auction. Standing on stage while people bid on you couldn't have been enjoyable.

"Now that you've satisfied your curiosity, what's new with you?" Duncan asked.

"Not much. Work is work, and my love life is nonexistent. It's as if every decent, single man has left New England."

Finding the right person could be difficult, and then other times, you met them when you least expected to. Tory glanced at Duncan. She certainly hadn't expected Duncan to be Mr. Right or at least Mr. Right for her. But it sure seemed to be the case.

"Do either of you have any single friends?" Harper asked, gesturing between Alec and Duncan.

"Not that I'd ever want you spending time with," Duncan answered without hesitation.

Harper frowned and stabbed a carrot with enough force to split it in half. "Do you have any brothers or sisters, Tory?"

"Two brothers, no sisters."

"Are they as overprotective and annoying as Duncan?"

Tory didn't even try to contain her smile. "Annoying, yes, especially Tyler, my younger brother. Adam wouldn't have wanted me to date his friends when we were younger, but he was never overprotective. And now he wouldn't care." She chose not to add that she had dated one of his friends. "But Adam is only a year and a half older than me. So it's a little different than you and Duncan." Tory couldn't imagine having a sibling who was either eleven years older or younger than her.

"Lucky you." She pointed her fork at Duncan. "This one acts like my second father. Sometimes he is worse than Dad."

"Hey, you're my sister, and I worry about you. And I'd do anything for you except set you up with my friends, who are too old for you anyway."

Harper tossed her napkin at Duncan, who threw it right back—something that would never happen around Shannon Sherbrooke's dinner table. "Tory, do you have any friends you could set me up with? I'd even settle for a cousin."

FIFTEEN

MANY OF THE ROOMS IN DUNCAN'S CONDO MIGHT BE OFF-WHITE like hers but not his bedroom. Nope, the four walls surrounding her were a rich cranberry color. One she could see in her place, although not in the bedroom. For her bedroom, she was leaning toward a shade of purple she'd found on an interior decorating website called *Romantic Moment*.

Readjusting the blankets, she turned her head toward Duncan. It did not surprise her he remained asleep. They certainly had gotten very little sleep last night. When they'd returned to the city yesterday evening and she'd gone to his place instead of hers, she'd planned to stay for a few hours and then head home. But sometimes, plans had a way of going off the rails.

Their last night in Puerto Rico and then again on Tuesday, they'd come close to having sex. In Puerto Rico, he'd ended things before they got that far, and on Tuesday, she had because the time hadn't felt right. Last night had been a different story. And Duncan must have sensed it, too, because he hadn’t tried to slow things down.

While the events of last night and early this morning had denied her sleep, they had provided her with clarity. All week she'd believed she was falling in love with Duncan. Now she knew she'd already fallen. She suspected the same might be true for Duncan. Until she was more confident about his feelings, though, she would keep her mouth shut. Some people got weird when others dropped the word "love" into a relationship. Duncan didn't seem like the type who would, but she'd rather be safe than sorry.

The body pressed against her side shifted, and an arm went across her stomach.

"Have you been awake long?" Remnants of sleep remained in Duncan's voice, and by the sound of it, he could easily fall back asleep.

"Just a few minutes."

"I wonder what time it is?" Duncan asked, kissing her bare shoulder.

The room contained various mementos and photos, but there wasn't a clock in sight. Her cell phone had never left her purse last night, and she didn't know where he'd left his.

"It's probably about time for us to get up." She'd love to spend the day where they were, but she'd told Judith they'd be there today. Tory didn't like to say one thing and then do another. Plus, she was looking forward to catching up with Leah and her other cousins. She just wished they expected her and Duncan next weekend instead of today.

Rather than get up, Duncan kissed her shoulder again. "It can't be that late."

"One of us could get up and check." Even if Duncan weren't cuddled up next to her, she wouldn't want to get up. She'd always found her bed comfortable, but it was a concrete slab compared to Duncan's mattress.

"I can take a hint," Duncan grumbled, moving into an upright position.

He didn't bother to pull on any clothes, and Tory enjoyed the view as he walked out of the room. Even before last night, she'd created an image of how he'd look naked. She hadn't been far off either. The man took care of himself. Duncan wasn't skinny like Grant, but he also wasn't overly muscular like Luke, who she'd always wondered if his physique was a combination of hours at the gym and steroids. Duncan was defined in all the right places, but it was clear he didn't spend every waking hour in a gym.

"Somehow, it's almost ten," he said, walking back into the room, his cell phone in hand. "What time do we have to be in Weston?"

"About twelve." Normally, she wouldn't worry about traffic as much on a Saturday, but this was the Saturday after Thanksgiving. So many people would be traveling to and from home or holiday shopping.

"That doesn't give us much time." Although Duncan sat, he didn't get under the covers next to her again. "It doesn't take me long to get ready, but I don't know how the traffic will be. If there isn't much, it should only take us about thirty minutes to get there. But there have been days when I've driven to the area for a meeting, and it's taken me over two hours. So we should probably get moving."

"That's what I was thinking." Sitting up, she leaned toward him and kissed him. "I'll meet you back down here when I'm ready." She didn't need five hours to get ready, but from what she'd seen in Puerto Rico, it would take her longer than him. And Duncan might as well be comfortable while he waited for her.

An hour and forty-five minutes later, Tory and Duncan walked into Judith's house. Size-wise, her parents' houses in Palo Alto and Healdsburg were equivalent. Somehow, though, this place felt more like a home and less like a showplace than Tory's parents'. And it had less to do with how the owners had decorated their homes. Rather, it was how Judith and Jonathan interacted with each other and anyone who visited.

It was apparent her cousin's parents loved each other. Tory's parents respected each other and got along well, but if they loved each other, they never showed it when others were around. She knew love hadn't factored into their decision to marry. Instead, it had been more like a business decision. Benjamin Sherbrooke Junior had wanted to purchase Desjardin Winery, and Shannon Desjardin had desired the Sherbrooke name and everything that went with it. Now they wanted her to follow in their footsteps of a loveless marriage by marrying Grant. Mom had even brought Grant up again when they spoke on Tuesday—a detail she'd left out when she told Duncan she'd spoken with her mom.

"I'm glad you both came today." After closing the front door behind them, Judith hugged her before doing the same to Duncan. "We're still waiting for Brett and Jen. They called us a little while ago to let us know there was an accident on 95 that has everything backed up. But everyone else is in the back living room. Make yourself comfortable. I'll be there in a minute."

Tory had spent enough holidays and weekends here while in high school to know where every room in the house was and how the family used them. For instance, the family only used the large picture-perfect living room off the main foyer when they hosted business dinners or fundraisers. The one in the back was where the family gathered day-to-day. Unlike the one most visitors saw, it contained family photos. The last time she'd visited, there had even been an entire collection of stuffed animals that belonged to Curt's daughter on a sofa. If her mom ever had grandchildren, she wouldn't let them leave their toys hanging around the house. At least, she'd never let Tory or her brothers do that. Instead, she'd insisted they stay either in their bedroom or their playroom unless they were outside toys. Then they went into the special toy shed.

Today, when they walked in, the two new school photos were the first thing Tory noticed. Reese, Curt's adopted daughter, and Erin, Leah's stepdaughter, might not be biologically related to Judith and Jonathan, but they treated them as if they were. A lot of people she knew, including many of her parents' friends, possibly even her parents, wouldn't be the same.

At the moment, the two girls sat together watching something on a tablet, and neither glanced in Tory and Duncan's direction as Tory made introductions.

Fifteen minutes later, Leah sat in the seat next to her. Bored with whatever they'd been watching on the tablet, Reese and Erin had convinced their dads and Duncan to go outside with them so Reese could show off some new soccer skill she'd been practicing.

"Duncan is a definite upgrade from Grant. Looks like the auction was a success for another Sherbrooke. Is it fair to assume he's the reason I haven't heard from you in weeks?" Leah asked.

"Him and Ivy's wedding."

"I forgot about the wedding. How was it? Was Grant a major pain in the butt?"

"It was the perfect wedding for Ivy and Preston." Her cousin didn't know Ivy super well, but she'd met her a bunch of times, and Tory had spoken about her, so Leah knew how much the couple loved the beach. "Grant wasn't as annoying as he could've been. Having Duncan there forced him to keep his distance."

"Hold on a minute, Duncan went with you? It sounds like things are moving fast between you two. I mean, the wedding was, what, three weeks after the auction?"

At the moment, they were the only ones in the room, but that could change at any moment. "When I bid on Duncan, I planned to ask him to come with me to the wedding and pretend to be my boyfriend." Even though the room was empty, she kept her voice close to a whisper.

"That doesn't sound like something you'd think up."

Tory shook her head. "I didn't. Ivy did." Come to think of it, she owed her friend a thank-you. If not for her outside-the-box crazy idea, she wouldn't be here with Duncan now.

"That makes more sense."

"Anyway, it never felt fake, even before we left for the wedding. Things between us progressed from there. I even joined his family Thursday for Thanksgiving. In two weeks, we're having dinner with my mom and dad."

"How did your parents take it when they found out you were with someone?" Leah asked.

Leah knew what Tory's parents wanted, and much like Tory, she couldn't figure out why.

"Mom wasn't thrilled. She called me at one o'clock in the morning after she found out from Mrs. Castillo. I haven't talked to Dad, but I'm sure he's not happy."

"Grant's mom should mind her own business."

Mrs. Castillo was a little nosey but still sweet. "I should've realized Grant's parents would be there and told Mom before she found out from someone else."

"How do you think it'll go when Benjamin and Shannon meet Duncan?"

Excellent question. Tory didn't expect her parents to be blatantly rude. That wasn't either one's style. But they wouldn't be warm and welcoming either. Not when, in their eyes, Duncan stood in the way of the outcome they wanted. Hopefully, they'd be polite and eventually come to welcome Duncan into their lives, because she didn't see him going anywhere.

Tory heard Reese and Erin's voices before they entered the room, followed by their fathers and Duncan.

"No idea," Tory answered.

ALTHOUGH JUDITH HADN'T PREPARED the meal, Thanksgiving dinner today was much more like the one she'd enjoyed with Duncan's family than any she'd experienced with her parents. After everyone finished eating, Reese and Erin convinced the younger guests, Tory and Duncan included, to join them outside for a soccer game. According to their fathers, both girls loved soccer. Although Tory wasn't the best player, a backyard game provided her with a way to burn off all the extra calories she'd get while eating dessert.

The moment they'd stepped outside, it'd been obvious how serious the two girls were about the sport. Two full-size nets occupied the yard. After they decided which goal would be theirs, the girls assigned the adults to a team and named themselves captains. Although it was only a backyard family game, the girls took every second seriously. They'd correct the players when they'd made a mistake and offer praise when they did something well. The two girls were natural leaders.

After exactly how long, Tory didn't know, the game ended; the final score was 2 to 1, with Reese's team winning. At first, the girls objected when told it was time to head inside. But then Curt reminded them that chocolate molten lava cakes were waiting inside, and they'd sprinted across the yard. Tory couldn't blame them. Chocolate molten lava cakes were yummy.

Now the two youngest guests were enjoying their second serving of dessert and once again watching something on Erin's tablet while the adults sat in small groups having their own conversations.

One particular group kept grabbing her attention. She couldn't say Duncan and Brett had been inseparable, but it seemed like when he wasn't with her, Duncan was with Brett. Sometimes Curt would be with them, and other times Gavin was with them. And once he'd even been talking with Brett and Harrison, Leah's uncle, who was a former United States senator.

Right now, Duncan, Curt, and Brett were sitting across the room, enjoying drinks and dessert.

"What about you, Tory?"

Jennifer's voice pulled Tory's attention back to the woman sitting near her.

"Sorry, my mind wandered."

Leah gave her a knowing smile. "Gee, I wonder where?"

Her cousin wasn't wrong. Her thoughts were on Duncan, just not in the way Leah thought. Duncan and her cousins could be discussing a million different things. But, unfortunately, every time she looked over and saw Duncan with Brett, she heard Grant's voice in her head.

"What was your question, Jen?" Tory forced her eyes to focus on Brett's wife rather than the men.

"Are you and Duncan going to the New Year's Eve party at Cliff House?"

For over a hundred years, the Sherbrookes had hosted a New Year's Eve party at Cliff House in Newport. Even though she received an invitation every year, she only sometimes attended. She hadn't thought about this year's upcoming party yet, but since she was already on the East Coast, it would be easy enough to go.

"Maybe. What about you guys?"

"Brett and I will be there," Jen answered.

"Curt and I will be in Florida with Mom and Reese," Taylor, Curt's wife, replied. "Reese doesn't know we're going yet."

"That sounds like fun. Erin has been after us to take her to Florida again," Leah said. "How long are you staying?"

"Nine days. You should see about coming with us. Reese and Erin would have a blast. They love spending time together."

While Leah and Taylor's conversation turned to how the girls got along a lot like sisters and how it was too bad they didn't live closer, Tory glanced in Duncan's direction again.

Much like earlier, Grant's words while they danced came back to haunt her, followed by Duncan's to his sister.

"You seem preoccupied. Is everything okay?" Leah nudged Tory's foot with hers.

"Just wondering what they're talking about." No way was she voicing what the real problem was to her best friend.

"Sports, maybe. It is football season," Jen said.

"Duncan's not all that much into football." Now, if it were baseball season, it would be a different story.

"It's probably something that would bore us to death, whatever it is," Leah said. "The last time Gavin and I went to Curt's, they spent over an hour discussing new solar-powered roof shingles some company designed. I don't remember the company's name. I thought I was going to fall asleep."

Across from her, Taylor cringed. "Yeah, I remember that. It was brutal. I tuned them out after a while.

Tory hoped they talked about something as dull as solar roof shingles or sports. A little voice that sounded an awful lot like Grant, though, kept telling her otherwise.

SIXTEEN

HE ALWAYS ENJOYED HIMSELF WHEN HE ATTENDED A Sherbrooke event. Today had been no different. But after sharing Tory with her relatives all day, he was looking forward to some time alone with her.

"Hi, Duncan, Tory."

He didn't need to turn around to know who'd entered the building's lobby behind them. He hadn't seen or heard from Lori Ann since Tory had her little chat with her in the locker room.

Lori Ann and someone he'd seen in the building's gym stopped next to them. Since the man had his arm around Lori Ann, Duncan guessed she'd finally given up on him and moved on to someone else.

About time.

"Do you know Isaac?" she asked, following Duncan and Tory into the elevator.

"I've seen him around, but we've never met." Duncan jabbed the button for his floor even though he and Tory hadn't discussed whose condo they were heading to tonight. Actually, they hadn't discussed what their plans were for the night or tomorrow. On the ride back, she talked more about Reese and Erin than anything else. They reminded her of her and Leah.

"Isaac and I are going to Bermuda next week. Didn't you two go there recently?" Lori Ann asked after making introductions.

"We went to Puerto Rico, but Bermuda is gorgeous too," Tory answered.

"I knew it was some island you went to this month. Going was Isaac's idea. We've both had enough of this cold weather."

All things considered, the weather had been mild for this month. The coldest day so far had been about thirty-two degrees.

The elevator stopped at the fourth floor, and the doors opened, thankfully putting an end to any further small talk.

"Have fun, and if we don't see you before then, have a great new year," Tory said as they exited the elevator.

He'd spent the day wanting to taste her again. Now that they were alone in his condo, he could do precisely that. Before she could remove her jacket, he pulled her against him and captured her lips with his. He started the kiss gently, more a brushing of his mouth against hers. Gradually he changed the intensity until she parted her lips, and his tongue met hers. With each pass, his internal temperature jumped another five degrees. Before he stripped them both naked right there, he pulled away and rested his forehead against hers as he tried to get his breathing back to normal.

"Stay here with me tonight."

Tory slipped from his embrace and removed her jacket. "We'll see. I haven't spent much time at home this week."

He could understand if she preferred to sleep in her bed. "We can go back to your place. It doesn't matter to me. I just want to be with you tonight."

"Maybe."

He let the issue go for now. Tory was hanging her jacket up, so she wasn't going anywhere now.

"Are you up for some television or a movie?" They'd started a movie trilogy that his cousin starred in last night but hadn't made it past the first movie.

In response, Tory shrugged, but since she walked toward his entertainment room, he took that as a yes.

"I didn't know Curt lived in Pelham." It had surprised him when Tory's cousin shared he and his family lived in the town next to the one he'd grown up in and where his parents still lived. "When I played Little League, we used to play against Pelham all the time."

"Yeah, I don't remember when he moved. But he's got a thing for remodeling old homes. The one he bought in Pelham is his most recent project, but I don't know if he's finished. I've never seen it."

"He invited us to visit the next time we're in the area. Maybe I should introduce him to my dad. They could share remodeling horror stories." He switched the television on as he put an arm across her shoulders. "Should we pick up with the next movie or try something else?" After all this time, you'd think he'd be used to seeing his cousin on the screen, but he still found it surreal.

"Whatever. Doesn't matter to me."

Last night she'd been adamant about what she would and wouldn't watch. Something was up. "What's wrong?"

Tory shrugged.

When you asked a question and got a shrug as the response, it was never a good sign. "Too much family time today?"

"No, I always enjoy getting together with my family. You got along well with everyone today. Every time I looked, it seemed you were with Brett and Curt."

Was she upset because he hadn't stuck to her like glue? That didn't seem like her.

"What did you guys talk about all day?"

"Nothing specific. Curt and I talked about the area where he lives, and then Brett mentioned he lives in North Salem. That is where my cousin CJ and his wife live. So we talked about the town a little. The Red Sox came up, and we talked about our families."

"Baseball season is over."

“We talked about game seven of the World Series last month. Harrison is almost as big a Red Sox fan as me. He has season tickets too.”

People would talk about that game for a long time. Boston had gone into the ninth down by five runs but somehow pulled off a win.

“You didn't talk about politics even once?”

“Yeah, it came up. When Brett asked about family, I mentioned Harper. He said he has an opening for a field representative, and he told me to have her apply. He's also willing to talk to her about running next year.”

“Well, isn't that convenient?” Tory crossed her arms, her jaw clenched tight.

He'd never heard her sound so frosty. “I'm not sure what you mean by that.”

“Your sister wants to enter politics, and you get to have lunch with a current United States Senator and a retired one.”

“I'd say it's a coincidence. Brett asked me about my family, I said I grew up in New Hampshire, Curt said he lived there now, and the conversation went from there.”

Rather than explain why she was upset, Tory studied him silently as he replayed the day in his mind. For the life of him, he didn't know what he'd done wrong. And if he wanted to know, he'd have to ask, because it didn't seem like she was about to tell him.

“Tory—”

“Why did you agree when I asked for your help after the auction?”

The conversation had stopped making sense to him several minutes ago.

“And be honest with me.”

“I thought you must be desperate if you asked me to pretend we were together.”

“That's the only reason?” she asked, sounding unconvinced.

"Yeah, what can I say? I enjoy helping people. Ask Alec or Matt. They'll tell you that."

Tory moved to the edge of the sofa, breaking contact. "I wish I believed that was the only reason."

"What the—" Duncan stopped and considered his words. "You haven't been yourself since we came in here. What's going on, Tory?" That sounded a little more diplomatic than what he'd almost said. "Do you think I agreed because of the donation you made to the animal shelter? I would've helped you even if you hadn't offered."

"No, I think you agreed because of my connections."

If she were into practical jokes, he'd think this entire conversation was a horrible one.

"Just like Grant and Luke," she added.

The only thing he had in common with Grant was they both had Y chromosomes and could easily pee standing up. He didn't know who Luke was, but he doubted he had anything else in common with him either.

He wanted to grab her shoulders and shake some sense into her; instead, Duncan dragged a hand through his hair. Where was her crazy thought coming from tonight?

"I don't know what happened between when we left here this afternoon and now, but how can you think I'm with you for your connections?"

"The other day, you told Harper you'd do anything for her at dinner. And then today, you conveniently work her into a conversation with Brett."

Had she bumped her head today when he wasn't looking? She was talking complete nonsense.

"Stop me if I get something wrong. When I agreed to help you, I secretly hoped our relationship would continue after the wedding so that I could use your connections and help my sister's political career. One that hasn't even started yet. Do you know how absurd that sounds?"

"People have done crazy things to get what they want. And

hey, you know what? We both got what we wanted, right? Grant more or less left me alone at the wedding. You helped your sister and got Lori Ann off your back."

Unable to sit any longer, he stood and walked toward the windows. When he reached them, he turned and walked back. "Everything you just said is bullshit."

He no longer cared about his word choice. "If I wanted a political connection, I could've asked Alec to introduce me to your cousin. Hell, I could've asked for an invitation to the New Year's Eve party in Newport so that I could talk to President Sherbrooke."

Duncan had only attended the party once, but according to Alec, his Uncle Warren had only missed the party twice in the past fifteen years, so there was an excellent chance he'd be there this year.

Tory's frown deepened. "I wish I believed that, Duncan. But I'm not sure I do. You wouldn't be the first man who wanted to be with me because of my political connections."

They had no future together if she didn't believe him, and he should ask her to leave. But first, he needed to get something off his chest.

"You're not the only one who's had people use you. I have. Both Alec and Matt have as well. It happens, and yeah, it sucks."

"Trust me, I realize that, but that doesn't change anything. We both got something out of our time together, and maybe it's time to go our separate ways."

A vise twisted in his chest, but he didn't argue with her or ask her to reconsider. If Tory believed this crap, she didn't know him at all.

"Maybe you're right."

TORY EXPECTED Duncan to follow her as she walked out of the entertainment room and grabbed her jacket. Even as she stood waiting for the elevator, she thought he'd come out and ask her to come back inside so he could continue to argue his case. When he didn't, it only reinforced the conclusion she'd reached. He didn't care about her. Grant had been right. Duncan was with her because of her connections, just like Grant and Luke. At least she'd figured it out sooner this time than when she'd been with Luke. Unfortunately, she'd learned the truth after falling in love with Duncan.

Tossing her jacket and purse on a chair in her condo, she pulled on the first pair of pj's her hand touched. Then, before leaving her bedroom, she grabbed her cell phone. A glance at the screen showed one message from her mom.

Not tonight.

She didn't feel like dealing with anyone tonight, especially her mother. But, rather than ignore the message, Tory replied, promising to call tomorrow, and then turned on the television. Maybe with a bit of luck, it would distract her until she fell asleep.

On the screen, the opening sequence to the newest *Lost In Space* played, but Tory barely noticed. Her mind kept replaying her and Duncan's time together, starting with the night of the auction and ending with their conversation tonight.

When she'd been with Grant and Luke, there had been signs of why they were with her. Unless she counted his conversation with her cousins today, she couldn't recall any signs with Duncan. Had he just been better at hiding the truth? Or had she overreacted?

Luke hadn't denied it when she confronted him and given him back the engagement ring. Instead, he'd gone on about how their relationship could benefit both of them. She hadn't addressed the matter with Grant when she ended their relationship, because their parents were such good friends, and she hadn't wanted to make things any more awkward than they were. Ivy's wedding had been the first time she mentioned it. Rather than refute her claim or go on about how they'd both benefit, he'd again come back with his standard "we belong together" line. Although their verbal responses differed, neither had been upset with her. Duncan was another story.

His disappointment and anger had been almost tangible. But was he upset because she'd figured out the truth, or because she had hurt him?

Last night when they'd made love, it had felt like more than a physical act. They'd seemed connected, as if they belonged together. She'd never experienced anything like it with anyone else. Then tonight, she'd seen the pain in his eyes.

Had she imagined the connection last night? Was Duncan as good an actor as his cousin? Or had she let Grant's words get to her and made a colossal mistake?

Answers to all three questions eluded her.

"If he cared, he would've tried harder to convince me I was wrong." But, even as she said the words, a counterargument formed.

What else could he have said that would've changed my mind?

Tory added it to her other unanswered questions. Ones she wouldn't answer tonight. Or maybe ever.

Leaning her head against the sofa, Tory wished she'd never taken Ivy's suggestion. Hell, she wished she'd never purchased the ticket and attended the stupid auction in the first place.

SEVENTEEN

Friday night, Tory stared into her tea. All week she'd focused on work, and when she wasn't doing that, she was on the computer either shopping for presents for the upcoming holiday or looking at various decorating sites for ideas. Her efforts had paid off, and she'd kept thoughts of Duncan at bay.

Maybe that was a bit of an exaggeration. She'd managed not to dwell on him all day long. But, at night, in her dreams, it had been a different story.

She had been successful in avoiding him, though. Of course, it helped that she'd worked from home three of the past five days, allowing herself to stay safely tucked away in her home office much of the week. She'd also avoided the gym and the pool just in case Duncan went down there.

But now she had nothing to distract her. If Leah or Ivy lived closer, she'd see if they wanted to get together. She'd already called Sienna, but she had plans with her sister tonight. She'd briefly considered calling her cousin Courtney, but she didn't feel like driving to Providence, leaving her with nothing to do but stare into her tea while reminding herself that thinking about Duncan was pointless.

Ever since she'd left his condo, whenever she received a text message or the phone rang, she picked up the device, expecting to see his name. Each time it wasn't him, disappointment struck, followed by the resolve that she'd made the right decision last weekend because his silence spoke volumes. He would've called or stopped by her place if he cared.

While her and Duncan's relationship had turned into a disaster, it had brought about one positive thing. Grant hadn't reached out to her even once. Whether that meant he'd accepted they weren't getting back together finally or he was just waiting until he knew she was single again, Tory didn't know. But since she was no longer seeing her parents next week, it would be a little while before Grant found out she and Duncan were no longer together.

She loved her parents, but it had been music to her ears when she learned their plans had changed. Now she could hold off until at least Christmas to tell them.

Tory drank the last of her lukewarm tea and stood. Hot tea might not solve her problems or ease the pain in her chest, but it didn't cause any new ones either. Plus, it sometimes helped her relax. She'd ingested a lot of tea this week. And while the first cup hadn't helped, maybe a second would do the trick tonight, because she desperately needed to relax.

The sound of wind chimes stopped her in the hallway. Like every other time she heard the sound this week, her heart stopped. Backtracking, she picked up her phone. When she saw the name Ivy on the screen, sadness and disappointment hit her like an eighteen-wheeler going a hundred miles an hour.

He hadn't called in almost a week. So why would he call now?

"Hey, Ivy." Tory headed back toward the kitchen. "How was the honeymoon?"

She didn't want to hear about Ivy and Preston's honeymoon right now, but it seemed like the appropriate thing to say since they hadn't spoken since the wedding.

"Fabulous. We didn't want to come home. Preston and I are already talking about going back in April."

Preston and Ivy traveled more than any of her other friends, so it did not surprise her there were already planning another getaway. However, their destination and when they planned to go was unexpected. They'd just spent two and a half weeks in Puerto Rico. She couldn't recall them ever visiting the same location twice in a year.

"Is the annual Nelson gathering not happening this year?"

For as long as Tory had known her, Ivy traveled to Florida for the Nelson family get-together in April.

"No, it's still happening. I'm not sure Preston and I are going this year. We saw everyone at the wedding."

"Have you told your parents yet?" Ivy's parents didn't agree on much, but they both believed family came first. She hadn't witnessed it, but she'd heard about their reaction the year Ivy's brother, Ted, skipped it.

"Yep, I told them last week."

"And the world didn't end?" For the first time all night, Tory wasn't thinking about Duncan.

Ivy laughed. "Hard to believe, I know. They weren't thrilled, but they seemed to understand. Although, of course, it might have helped they learned Madeline is pregnant the same day."

"I guess it wasn't a lucky accident that you told your parents the same day your brother shared his news?"

"You know me so well. Ted called me before our parents."

Ivy's statement didn't surprise her. Maybe it was because they were twins, but Ted and Ivy were close and always had been. Even when Preston proposed, Ivy called her brother, followed by Tory, before her parents.

"How are things going for you?" Ivy asked, making the conversation about Tory instead.

"Work is great, and I'm almost done with my Christmas shopping. I also have some ideas about how I want to decorate the condo."

"Well, that's great, but not where I was going with my question."

Yeah, I know that.

"How are things going with Duncan?"

"They're not. We haven't spoken since last Saturday."

"Oh." Silence followed the one-word reply, but it wouldn't last, not with Ivy on the other end of the line.

"What happened?"

"Either I overreacted, or Duncan falls into the same category as Grant and Luke."

Tory filled Ivy in on everything while she prepared her tea. And in true Ivy fashion, she freely gave her opinion of Grant and where he should shove his thoughts. It really was too bad Grant was Preston's cousin.

"What do you think?" Tory asked when she finished.

Maybe Ivy could provide some insight into the matter. However, it might not matter anyway. If she'd been right about Duncan, she wanted nothing to do with him. And if she'd made a mistake, he might be unwilling to forgive her. If the latter was the case, she couldn't blame him. No one appreciated being accused of something untrue.

"Honestly, Duncan didn't seem like the type to use someone like that, but I spent little time with him. Some people are good at hiding their true intentions."

"You're not being very helpful." Truthfully, she wasn't being helpful at all.

"You didn't let me finish."

"Sorry, I'm listening," Tory said before sipping her tea.

"It is possible you're 100 percent right about him. He might have planned from the beginning to manipulate things so you'd stay together after the wedding."

When they'd spent time together, it never felt as if Duncan was steering their relationship in a particular direction. But the best manipulators kept their victims in the dark.

"It seems like a stretch to me," Ivy continued. "But what I

think, or anyone else, doesn't matter. You need to decide. Maybe you should try writing everything down."

She always found it helpful to write things down when she had a problem. And she would've thought to do it already if she hadn't been so focused on not thinking about Duncan.

When no paper turned up in the kitchen drawers, Tory carried her tea into her office.

"How do you think I should organize it?" she asked, turning on the desk lamp. A traditional pros and cons list didn't fit the situation.

"No idea. You're the list maker, not me."

Ivy's comment brought to mind the list of questions she made weeks ago—the ones Duncan had answered without a single complaint.

"Do you mind if I call you back later?" Tory asked.

Right now, it was more about getting her thoughts and feelings on paper than about organization.

"You better, or I'll call you."

"YOU REALLY SHOULDN'T LEAVE your door unlocked," Gianna said in lieu of a greeting when she and Alec walked into the kitchen.

When he'd learned they were going to a concert tomorrow afternoon at the Garden, he'd invited them to spend the weekend with him. While Duncan wanted to catch up with his favorite cousin and best friend, it wasn't the only reason he'd invited them. He hoped the company would keep his thoughts off Tory, because work certainly hadn't.

Much like when they'd been in high school, he'd looked for her each time he left his condo, but the only place he'd seen her had been in his mind—a place he tried to banish her from, because thinking about her accomplished nothing. Unfortunately, he failed more than he succeeded. Thoughts of their last conversation hit him at least once a day. When that wasn't replaying itself, memories of their time together paraded through his mind.

When Tory had walked out on Saturday, he'd almost followed her. He even made it to the door. But, ultimately, he'd decided he'd be better off giving her some space. Once she had time to think about everything, she'd realize how wrong she was and come to him. Duncan no longer saw that happening—not after six days—and he would not beg her.

"Thanks for the advice, Mom." Duncan pulled her into a bear hug.

"You know he does it because he's too lazy to walk to the door every time someone rings the bell." Alec dropped one of the suitcases he held and helped himself to a mozzarella stick.

"Why am I not surprised?" Gianna said, returning Duncan's embrace.

"Do you care which room we stay in this weekend?"

"You pick."

"I'll be right back." Alec kissed Gianna on the cheek before walking away.

He never imagined his cousin and best friend getting together, but they were obviously happy together.

"Do you need help with anything?" Gianna asked.

The menu for tonight was typical poker game food: easy, and except for the veggie platter, not all that healthy.

"You can grab the veggie platter from the fridge," he answered, opening the oven and removing the meat lover's pizza —just one of the four types he'd bought.

"What time are Matt and Tory getting here?"

"I'm here now." Matt and Alec entered the kitchen at the same time. "And since Alec's here with you, I see you're still babysitting him. But if you ever get tired of doing it, you know where to find me."

"That would be like going from babysitting a six-year-old to a two-year-old." Giving his friends a hard time was just the thing Duncan needed tonight.

"I don't know, Duncan," Gianna countered. "I think Alec has the maturity of at least an eight-year-old. You, on the other hand, I'm not so sure about. Maybe I'll discuss it with Tory when she gets here."

Duncan ignored his cousin's last comment. "You can think about it while we play cards." Since there was no baseball game tonight, he'd set everything up in the kitchen instead of the entertainment room. "This isn't a restaurant. Help yourself." Grabbing a plate, he added some of everything to it. "What should we play tonight?"

Most often, they played Texas Hold'em, but occasionally, they wanted a change and played seven-card stud or five-card draw.

"Shouldn't we wait for Tory, or is she not coming?" Gianna asked as she sat across from him.

"Just the four of us tonight. Tory and I aren't together anymore."

His cousin's eyebrows bunched together, and he knew she wouldn't let his comment go. "I didn't expect that. You guys seemed close on Thanksgiving. What happened?"

The three people at the table didn't need all the details.

Never one to pass up an opportunity to give him a hard time, Matt spoke up before Duncan answered. "She realized she could do better."

"You're not funny," Gianna said, glaring at Matt.

"Well, he's funny-looking." Although they had yet to decide on which poker style they were playing, Alec shuffled the cards.

Gianna nodded. "I can't argue with you there."

"Tory and I decided it wasn't working."

His cousin studied him and slightly shook her head. "I noticed the way you looked at her last week. There's more to it than it wasn't working. But if you don't want to share, that's fine."

Of course Gianna would know he was holding something back, but he didn't want to get into it tonight—or maybe ever.

"Is everyone good with Texas Hold'em tonight?" The sooner they focused on something other than his love life, the better.

Five hours later, Duncan sat watching television with his cousin while Alec slept with his head in Gianna's lap. After Matt left, his wallet much lighter than when he walked in, thanks to Gianna, the three of them gathered in the entertainment room. Halfway through the first episode of a series they all liked, Alec fell asleep. He hadn't made a sound since.

"I'm going to get a drink. Do you want me to get you anything, so you don't have to disturb Sleeping Beauty?" Duncan gestured toward his friend as he stood.

"Can you get me a root beer if there are any left or a seltzer water?"

"I'll see what I have."

Operating under the old saying, out of sight, out of mind, he'd left his cell phone in his bedroom when he came home tonight. As he walked back to the other room, he considered making a detour and checking to see if he had any messages from Tory.

It's not going to happen. So rather than face disappointment, Duncan kept going.

"Here you go." He handed his cousin the can and then returned to his spot and unpaused the show.

For a few minutes, the only sound came from the sound system speakers. But the way Gianna kept looking at him instead of the screen told him that wouldn't be the case for long.

"Since Matt is gone and Alec's asleep, do you want to talk about Tory?"

"There's not much to talk about, Gi."

"I don't believe you. You wouldn't have brought her to the island twice and introduced her to everyone if you didn't care a lot about her. So what happened between last week and today? Maybe I can help."

Gianna meant well. "There is no way anyone can help. Tory believes I was with her for her connections."

"That makes no sense. Why would she think that?"

Since it was easier than getting her to drop the matter, Duncan shared his and Tory's last conversation. Tonight, like then, he didn't understand how she could believe that about him.

"People make mistakes. Tory might realize she did and come around."

He didn't see that happening. "Even if she does, in my experience, most people won't admit when they're wrong." Duncan raised his glass to his mouth so his cousin wouldn't see his frown.

"If she cares enough, she will. I did this summer with Alec."

His cousin caught his attention with that comment, and since she was prying into his life, he'd do the same. Swallowing his water, Duncan put the glass down. "What mistake did you make?"

Gianna closed her eyes as she pinched the bridge of her nose, a clear sign she wished she'd kept her mouth shut. "Alec never told you what happened?"

"Nope." If he had, Duncan wouldn't be asking now.

Sighing, she looked at him. "Right before Alec started working at the foundation, I assumed some things about him and ended our relationship."

"Whatever it was, you could've called me, and I would've told you that you were wrong." The only person he knew better than his cousin was Alec.

"It doesn't matter," she said, shrugging a shoulder. "I realized I was wrong. Give Tory some time. She might too."

He'd give her all the time she wanted, but he didn't believe she'd change her mind.

"Do you want to watch another episode or call it a night?" Duncan had answered Gianna's questions and was done with the topic.

"I'm going to bed as soon as this one is over."

Not eager for dreams of Tory again, Duncan remained on the sofa when Alec and Gianna left. An hour later, though, his body didn't care what Duncan wanted, and he headed to his room. The cell phone on the bureau called out to him as he undressed, and he grabbed it on his way to the bathroom.

The message on the screen stopped him in his tracks.

If you're around, can we talk?

Tory had sent the message at seven thirty. If it hadn't been after midnight, he'd call her.

Sorry. I'm just seeing this now. I'll be around tomorrow.

He'd hear her out if she wanted to talk and then go from there.

EIGHTEEN

It hadn't taken Tory long to realize the colossal mistake she'd made once she'd started writing things down. She'd like to attribute it to Grant. If not for their conversation, she wouldn't have questioned Duncan's motives. However, she couldn't blame it all on him. She'd let her insecurities prevail over her common sense, not something that usually happened to her.

Realizing she'd messed up was one thing. Getting Duncan to forgive her and give their relationship another try was something else. Honestly, she wouldn't blame him if he refused.

Or maybe he already has.

Last night, after she'd mentally kicked her butt for being such an idiot and called herself every name in the book, she'd sent him a text. With the ball in his court, she'd waited for a response —one that never came before she went to bed. Perhaps he needed time to think. It was also possible his silence was his answer, and he'd spent the night with another woman.

Although warm in bed, she needed to use the bathroom, and she was hungry. Tory, unfortunately, couldn't solve either problem from the comfort of her bed. Before she addressed the first issue, Tory pulled on the bathrobe she'd tossed on the bed last night and stuck her cell phone in the pocket.

She paused on her way through the living room, surprised by the oversized, fluffy snowflakes hitting the window. Since she had no weekend plans, she hadn't checked the forecast all week. However, a glance outside told her the snow had been falling for a little while.

Just how much were they going to get? Stepping away from the window, Tory pulled out her cell so she could check the weather app as she headed toward her original destination.

Duncan's message greeted her and kept her from looking at anything else. According to the timestamp, he'd sent it at a quarter to one this morning. Had he not seen her message until then because he'd been out with someone? If so, she only had herself to blame. Or was that just an excuse and he'd needed time to decide if he wanted to talk to her?

Does it matter? He hadn't told her to get lost. He must be open to talking if he'd said he was around today. It was a start, and she'd take it.

She wanted to call him now, but if he'd still been up at almost one o'clock, who knew when he'd gone to bed? So instead, she'd have breakfast and get ready for the day before reaching out again. Hopefully, by then, he'd be up as well and ready for a visitor.

Tory managed a bowl of oatmeal and two cups of coffee before pulling up Duncan's contact information.

Is there a good time I can see you today?

She drummed her fingertips against the table and started on her third coffee. Seconds that felt more like hours passed before a response appeared.

Whenever you want.

She took that as a promising sign.

Can I come by now?

Alec and Gi are here. I'll come to you. Give me 15.

Sounds good.

She'd prefer privacy for this conversation, and it would take him just as long to get to her as it would for her to go down to his place.

She wasn't usually a pacer. Now she went between pacing and drumming her fingers against the counter while she waited —all the while asking herself the same questions.

Would he meet with her if there was no chance of them getting back together? Was he coming up just to hear her say she'd been wrong? Some people would do that. When she finished, would he turn around and leave?

Lost in thought, Tory jumped half a mile when the doorbell rang.

This is it.

"Hey, come in." Her initial instinct was to put her arms around him, but she'd lost that right Saturday night. So instead, she clasped her hands behind her back and watched him close the door behind him. "Can I get you anything?"

"All set. We were eating breakfast when you texted me."

She should've waited longer. "Are Alec and Gianna spending the weekend?"

"Yeah, they got here last night. We were playing poker with Matt when you texted me yesterday. That's why I didn't see it until later."

Well, at least he hadn't been with someone else. "That's okay. I, uh, let's sit down."

He didn't touch her as he followed her, but her body prickled at his proximity as it remembered waking up next to him last weekend. Now, if she turned, she could press her body to his and slip her fingers through his hair while kissing him.

Focus on one thing at a time. Before Tory did anything, she needed to clear the air between them. And even though sitting next to Duncan was detrimental to her concentration, she joined him on the sofa.

"I'm sorry, Duncan." She hadn't rehearsed what she'd say, but it never hurt to start with an apology when you made a mistake, especially one as colossal as hers. "I let what Grant said to me get into my head last weekend. It shouldn't have happened, but it did."

"Why would you listen to anything he says?" Duncan asked, his expression unreadable, but at least he was talking to her. "The man is only after what is best for him."

Tory rubbed her palms against her thighs. "I didn't at first. But then I found out about your sister wanting to go into politics and saw you talking to Brett all day." She dragged her teeth across her bottom lip, well aware of how stupid she'd been. "Everything snowballed from there. Both Grant and Luke, my ex-fiancé, wanted to be with me because it benefited them. And I lumped you in with them, which I shouldn't have done. It wasn't fair to you, and if I could go back in time and change things, I would." Especially the part about ever getting involved with Grant or Luke.

Leaning forward, Duncan rested his forearms on his thighs. "There are a lot of people in the world like Grant. I've dealt with a few too. But there are a lot more who aren't like them. You cannot assume everyone wants to use you because of two jerks."

She'd apologized, and he hadn't pulled her close and kissed her. He also hadn't walked out either.

"Rationally, I know that. But, emotionally, well, it can be tricky, Duncan."

"Understandable." Duncan wrapped a finger around her pinkie. "So, where does that leave us?"

He used the word "us." That has to be a good sign, right?

"I'd like things to return to the way they were before last Saturday night. But I understand if that's not possible. Things between us moved fast." In a month, they'd gone from mere acquaintances to lovers. "If you want to start over and go slow, we can. And if you want nothing else to do with me, I'll respect that too."

A lump formed in her throat at the thought of Duncan leaving her life for good. And while it would hurt like hell, she'd respect his decision because she'd brought the whole crappy situation on herself.

"I would've already left if that was what I wanted." He moved closer and laced his fingers through hers. "But I need you to trust me. If we're going to work, I need you to say something if you're having doubts, so we can talk about it before things snowball as they did."

After this weekend, she didn't see Grant's comments or her insecurities affecting their relationship again. "I can do that." Placing her palm on his cheek, she lowered her mouth to his. "I've missed you so much this week."

Tory hoped her lips conveyed the thoughts going through her head. She would not assume that was the case. Ending the kiss, she rested her forehead against his.

"I love you."

Duncan pulled back and met her eyes, the smile on his face telling her everything she needed to know. Even though she'd been an idiot, he loved her too.

"I'm glad we're on the same page."

DUNCAN PUT his arm around Tory when she sat down again and pressed play on the remote control. On the television, Indiana Jones waded through rats under the city of Venice in search of a medieval knight's burial site.

Rather than deal with the crummy weather, the four of them had decided to spend the evening at home. Unable to agree on a new movie, they'd turned to his classic collection. The first three movies in the Indiana Jones series were the only ones that earned everyone's vote. They had already finished the first two and were on *Indiana Jones and The Last Crusade*. Although his favorite, Duncan wasn't paying attention to the movie. Instead, he was thinking about his and Tory's conversation earlier, especially the part about her ex-fiancé. Surprise had been the first emotion he'd experienced when he'd learned she'd been engaged a few years ago. Anger had replaced it when he'd learned what an ass the guy had turned out to be. After meeting Grant and hearing about Luke, he now had a better understanding of where Tory's insecurities had come from.

"All the answers to every mystery in the universe could be down there and you still wouldn't find me in a place like that," Gianna said, pulling him from his thoughts. His cousin could handle mice, snakes, and any insect that came her way, but rats were a different story.

Duncan didn't entirely agree with her. He wasn't a fan of rats either, but depending on the treasure, he'd wade through them like the character was now. But it would have to be one hell of a treasure.

"Yeah, I'm not sure which would be worse, rats or snakes. Just watching the scene in *Raiders of the Lost Ark* made my skin crawl," Tory said.

He'd noticed she'd looked away from the television when the hero and heroine got sealed underground with the snakes. As a general rule, snakes didn't bother him. He had his job every summer working for Uncle Corey to thank for that. You couldn't work as a landscaper and not come across snakes. Of course, the snakes on Sanborn Island were harmless, making it easy to deal with them.

"Snakes don't bother me. Still, I wouldn't want to be sealed up with thousands of them," Gianna said, checking her beeping cell phone.

"Is everything okay?" Alec asked.

"It's a weather alert." With a job so weather-dependent, Gianna had her phone set up to receive regular weather updates. "You might be stuck with us an extra day, Duncan. They don't expect this storm to move out of the area until tomorrow evening."

The snow had been off and on throughout the morning and early afternoon. Since Alec and Gianna returned from their concert, though, it hadn't stopped. Instead, it and the wind had picked up in intensity, and it wouldn't surprise Duncan if the city lost power.

"You're always welcome here, Gi. You know that." Duncan gestured toward Alec. "He, on the other hand, is another story."

Alec lifted his head off Gianna's lap, which he'd been using as a pillow. "Duncan, you're not fooling anyone here. We all know you love me."

"Keep telling yourself that." Duncan winked at his cousin. "I only keep you around because you make Gianna happy."

"I appreciate the sacrifice, Duncan. Truly I do," Gianna said, somehow managing not to smile.

With no good response, Duncan went back to watching the movie. His thoughts quickly turned away from it again and to the people around him. Life didn't get much better than this. He had his favorite cousin and his closest friend sitting to his left, and the woman he loved snuggled up against him. When he'd made the bet with Alec months ago, he'd never imagined this would be the outcome. But he wouldn't complain about the unexpected turn of events. Hell, right up until he walked on stage, he'd been kicking himself for making the stupidest bet of his life. But, in reality, it turned out to be the best thing he'd ever done for both him and Alec.

Duncan didn't care if they had company. Leaning toward her, he kissed her. "I love you."

The dimple he loved so much appeared in her right cheek when she smiled. "Love you too."

ABOUT THE AUTHOR

USA Today Best Selling author, Christina Tetreault started writing at the age of 10 on her grandmother's manual typewriter and never stopped. Born and raised in Lincoln, Rhode Island, she has lived in four of the six New England states since getting married in 2001. Today, she lives in New Hampshire with her husband, three daughters and two dogs. When she's am not driving her daughters around to their various activities or chasing around the dogs, she is working on a story or reading a romance novel. Currently, she has four series out, The Sherbrookes of Newport, Love on The North Shore, Elite Force Security and her newest The Sherbrookes. You can visit her website or follow her on Facebook to learn more about her characters and to track her progress on current writing projects.

OTHER BOOKS BY CHRISTINA

Loving The Billionaire

The Teacher's Billionaire

The Billionaire Playboy

The Billionaire Princess

The Billionaire's Best Friend

Redeeming The Billionaire

More Than A Billionaire

Protecting The Billionaire

Bidding On The Billionaire

Falling For The Billionaire

The Billionaire Next Door

The Billionaire's Homecoming

The Billionaire's Heart

Tempting The Billionaire

The Billionaire's Kiss

A Billionaire's Love, a novella

The Irresistible Billionaire

The Courage To Love

Hometown Love

The Playboy Next Door

In His Kiss

A Promise To Keep

When Love Strikes

Her Forever Love

Born To Protect

His To Protect

Love And Protect

One Of A Kind Love

Unexpectedly In Love

Made in the USA
Coppell, TX
02 December 2024

41523639R00125